Monsoon
and Other Stories

Arinn Dembo

Kthonia Press
Vancouver, British Columbia
www.kthonia.com

All rights reserved. No part of this publication may be reproduced, stored in a retrieval system, or transmitted in any form or by any means, electronic, mechanical, photocopying, recording or otherwise, without the prior written permission of the publisher.

Text Copyright © 2011 Arinn Dembo
Design Copyright © 2011 Kthonia Press Cooperative

Cover art by Ashley Walters

This book is also available in electronic form.

Library and Archives Canada Cataloguing in Publication

Dembo, Arinn, 1970-
    Monsoon and other stories / Arinn Dembo.

Short stories.
Also issued in electronic format.
ISBN 978-0-9877496-1-1

    I. Title.

PS8607.E52M65 2012   C813'.6   C2012-900641-6

Dedication

This book is dedicated to all things divine and depraved—
including you, my love.

Table of Contents

Acknowlegdments 7
Monsoon.. 9
Severity... 25
Sisterhood of the Skin... 27
The Humanist's Prayer 45
We Are Indra 47
The Other Wife.. 51
The Foreordained Rabbit 55
Indigestion.. 59
Three Desert Poems 65
ICHTHYS 69
Back to Back (A Valentine's Day Poem) 87
The Words.. 89
The Crown... 109
Sacred Heart.. 117
Maybe... 133
When Push Comes to Shove 137
The Passenger.. 145
The Zombie's Prayer 153
About the Author.. 157

Acknowlegdments

The author would like to thank the editors, publishers and contest judges who first chose to print some of the short stories and poems which are re-printed in this volume. "Sisterhood of the Skin" first appeared in *The Magazine of Fantasy and Science Fiction,* June 1996. "We are Indra" was published in *Radiant Reason: the New Humanism* in 1999. "Severity" and "Three Desert Poems" first appeared in the *Raindrops Literary Review* in 1999, and "The Crown" followed in 2001. "The Humanist's Prayer" appeared in *The Manitoba Humanist* in 2004. "Indigestion" and "When Push Comes to Shove" were first written as entries for the *Vancouver Courier*'s annual fiction contest and published with other prize winners of that contest. "Monsoon" was the first-prize winner of the Best Fantastic Erotica contest sponsored by Circlet Press in 2006, and first appeared in the anthology of the same name published in December 2007. "The Other Wife" was published in *H.P. Lovecraft's Magazine of Horror* in 2006 and "ICHTHYS" was published in the same magazine in 2009.

Additional thanks as always to Bob Kruger and Silvia Moreno-Garcia, the seasoned professionals at Electric Story and the Innsmouth Free Press respectively, who helped prepare this text for publication in electronic and print formats. Artist and graphic designer Ken Lee also deserves a word of thanks for the artistic eye and consummate skill he brings to all projects, large and small.

Monsoon

It was June in Maharashtra, and the monsoon would not come. The whole district lay panting in the heat, the burning sky clapped tight overhead like the lid of a tandoor oven. Lean goats stumbled down the narrow alleyways, udders hanging slack and dry beneath them; beggars cried for water in every village. Dust-devils swept over baked clay and through the dry weeds, whistling and shrieking. Hot sand blew into the eyes of torpid bullocks as they leaned into the yoke, whips snapping over their bony backs. A single stream crept along the valley floor, shrunken and muddy, and women stood ankle deep in its shallows, beating their laundry against rocks that rippled and danced in the sun.

Benton watched those women from behind his mirror shades, their saris wringing wet and clinging like crepe to their bodies. The trip to Wainganga by Jeep was long, particularly in a Jeep so old and decrepit as this one; any distraction from the heat and the choking clouds of dust was welcome.

He held up his fist abruptly and Charanjit brought the vehicle to a shuddering, squealing halt by the side of the road, burying the two men briefly in a whirlwind of fine grit. "How long, my friend?" the driver asked. He turned his wrist proudly, showing off the glittering face of a new watch.

"*Das*," Benton said, climbing out of the passenger seat with his cameras swinging around his neck. He could speak relatively decent Hindi, and Charanjit's English was impeccable, but the two men chose to communicate in monosyllables and hand signals more often than not; they had worked together before. Charanjit would now wait ten minutes before he began to lean on the horn imperiously, demanding that Benton return.

The white man limped down the hill toward the water, his right leg aching and stiff with travel. The women continued their work in the riverbed; he crouched beside a thorn bush and took several pictures of them, focusing his lens on wet bellies ... brown breasts ... flexing thighs ... streaming, sopping masses of black hair. It was a prosperous family, the daughters plump and smooth.

The shutter clicked and whirred like the wings of a locust. One of the younger girls looked up suddenly and saw him across the river. Her black eyes flashed. Just moments before her voice rang out in warning, Benton captured one last perfect image of her face, her pale pink tongue-tip passing over the ripe curve of her upper lip. Then all the women were standing, laughing, scowling, chattering to one another in Hindi... all the while drawing the folds of their wet saris about them, arms crossed over their conical breasts to fend off his camera.

He turned away and went back to the Jeep, half-staggering on the incline. The passenger seat had been repaired so many times with silver duct tape that none of the original upholstery could be seen. Benton sat down heavily, letting his long, lean body drop into the burning chair. He massaged his aching thigh absently and drew his filthy red bandanna up to cover his mouth; the taste of dust was thick on his tongue, but he could not slake his thirst here.

ଔ ଔ ଔ

Benton had been dry since Mombasa. His original plan had been to stop in the Old Town there. Among those twisting alleys there was an oasis where the caramel-colored daughters of the Faithful could be bought as easily as a dish of fried *casava* or a handful of sticky dates; it was one of his favorite haunts in the city. He liked the kohl-rimmed eyes of the dancers, lustrous and burning over their filmy veils. In the leaping shadows of the back room, he had drawn aside those veils more than once to kiss the forbidden lips of a Moslem girl.

Time had not allowed for his little diversion, however, and once again in Mumbai it was the same: no brothels, just an endless hurry through passport offices and transit bureaus to get his papers in order. As the Jeep jounced and rattled along the dirt road, Benton counted the days since he had laid hands on a woman.

Half the reason for his choice of profession was the love of women; he always devoured them greedily when he was abroad. He couldn't capture the flavor of a place until he made love there. The women were as inseparable from the mystique of a foreign land as its music, its language, its liquor and food. Every country offered a subtle variation on the eternal flavor—he sampled them all, like the alien fruit and curry in the marketplace.

The women he could not bring to his bed, he collected with his camera. If possible, he would always do both. He was paid to take pictures of mountains, rivers, rice paddies and ruins—but it was his dream someday to publish his thousands of photos of women. He would present the beauties of the world, all the bright vivid creatures from Mandalay to Manhattan: they would be his gift to the Arts.

For now, however, he was simply suffering, and it seemed that the whole earth was suffering with him. The sere hills of Pusad gave way to the Upper Bhima Valley and then the plain of Nagpur, a broad flat slab that stretched for miles in the blinding sun. The wind roared like a furnace at the nape of his neck. Dead, brittle cotton still stood in the fields; dry leaves rattled, and stinging dust slashed across the faces of water-bearers walking by the side of the road. The women and boys were black and thin beneath their ceramic jars, their arms and legs bent like wrought iron.

When the Jeep passed a town, there were always red-eyed men taking shelter in doorways, sitting on overstuffed sacks and smoking. Water salesmen pedaled along the streets, selling a single drink for three rupees. A sudden gust would turn the sky the color of dried blood; weak, irritable-looking mothers looked out their windows at the passing shadow, holding listless babies in their arms and searching the sky for clouds.

Just a few miles from Darwha, the engine began to make an ominous hiss. Charanjit clucked nervously and continued on, egging the reluctant machine into the next village while the water steadily boiled away. When at last he rolled to a stop, he reached across Benton's lap to open the glove compartment, unwinding the piece of rusty wire that held it shut.

"No problem," he said, giving Benton a cheery smile. He took out a pair of oven mitts.

The photographer shook his head, disgusted.

"No problem," Charanjit repeated. He hurried around to the grill of the Jeep, putting on his oven mitts, and unlatched the hood. Steam rushed out at him in a cloud.

Benton climbed out after him. Standing beside Charanjit, he waved the billowing steam away and bent to inspect the damage. Even from this angle, he could see a long crack in the radiator; the last drops of water and antifreeze sizzled, slowly oozing from the breach and boiling away on black metal.

He straightened up, took off his baseball cap and raked a tangle of dark, sweaty hair away from his brow. "No problem," he said sarcastically.

"My apologies, Joseph." Charanjit was shamefaced. "I had hoped it was only the hose."

Benton sighed, looking around him. The two men were standing in the middle of an open square. In the shelter of the buildings across the way, there was a scanty village market—a few blankets spread out on the ground, each covered with merchandise. Children were already gathering in a loose semi-circle around the Jeep, smiling shyly at Charanjit. As Benton limped away, they began pelting the friendly driver with questions.

Irritable and thirsty, Benton unscrewed his lens cap, looking for a target. An old woman caught his eye in the dust of the market; she was sitting perfectly still and straight against a mud wall. Her hair hung down to her waist, gray as ashes, and her sari was dark chocolate brown. Bright gold flashed from her hands, her feet, her neck and wrists.

He approached cautiously, making his way through the crowd toward her. She sat beside a blanket spread with shallow wooden bowls, each one filled with something different. He looked down at them, fascinated by the array of colors: deep, dark chili powder and golden brown turmeric; lentils in black, yellow, scarlet and green; sugar, salt, rice; peppercorns and cardamoms; beans and fennel; cloves and saffron and sticks of cinnamon.

The old woman herself was blind, her enormous eyes blanketed by silvery cataracts. What a face she had! The bones were sharp and delicate, still curving exquisitely beneath her withered skin—the foundation of a great aquiline beauty, heart-ripping in its youth. Rings glittered on every twig-like finger and toe; a golden serpent wound around her neck, biting its own tail. Benton squatted in the dust a few feet away and snapped a picture of her.

Instantly she turned toward him, a quick avian flick of the head. "Five rupees," she said, in English.

"For what?" he asked, startled.

"For my picture, sir." She spoke English with an accent; it sounded as if she had learned the language from a Scotsman. "Surely a rich tourist does not rob a poor old Indian woman?"

"Five rupees? For a picture?" He grinned. "I'm the one getting robbed!"

She smiled thinly. "One must live."

He unbuttoned the front pocket of his shirt and pulled out a handful of coins. "What if I want pictures of your *daal* and *dalchini* as well, mother?" he said in Hindi, rattling the money in his hand.

"For six rupees, everything." She made a magnanimous sweep of her hand over her blanket and wares, smiling again, more warmly this time. Again he saw the ghost of the girl she must have been, and she tugged at his heart. "I will give you a cinnamon stick, to show that I am not ungenerous."

The bargain made, Benton squatted and photographed her from a variety of angles, putting the curling tube of brown bark in the corner of his mouth like a cigarette while he did his work. Just as he was rising, a little boy ran up to him, wearing a pair of ragged shorts and a short-sleeved cotton shirt.

"Here, mis-tah," he said in English. He thrust out his hand; he was holding a fat little plastic bag, filled with green shaved ice. There was a rubber band holding it shut at the top, and a drinking straw poked deep into the middle. He waved vaguely at the crowd behind him with his free hand, smiling widely. "*Mem sahib* sends this to you, with her com-ple-ments."

Benton looked over the boy's shoulder for a mother or sister standing somewhere in the marketplace, but none of the women there seemed to be paying attention. "What is it?" He looked down at the little bag suspiciously.

"*Nimbu pani*," the boy said. He held out his hand again, huge black eyes pleading. "It is very good; please try!"

Temporarily unable to remember what the Hindi words meant, Benton took the sweating bag reluctantly and put the straw to his lips. He took a tiny sip; ice-cold limeade burst on his palate, sharp and sweet.

Seeing the expression on his face, the boy smiled broadly. "Good, yes?"

Benton chuckled and reached into his pocket for coins. "Very good. How much does she charge for these?"

The boy waved his hands no, black eyes sparkling. "*Mem sahib* has paid already, mis-tah. I will have one for myself and five rupees too, now I have given it to you!"

The boy turned and ran away, wriggling through the press of the marketplace. Benton tried to watch where he went for a few moments, to see if he could spot his benefactress among the villagers … but there was only a glint of blue and silver in the shadowed archway where the boy had disappeared, and a flash that could have been a pale hand.

The photographer passed the bag of ice over his forehead and cheeks, and then drank more deeply from the straw, filling his mouth with chilly sour-sweet. Charanjit had disappeared briefly into a shop across the square; now he was returning with a purposeful stride.

"There is a mechanic here." He jerked a thumb over his shoulder. "He does not have a radiator for us, but he is traveling tonight to Darwha. I will go with him, buy the part from the dealer, and return tomorrow morning. We will be on the road again before midday."

Benton sighed. "And what am I supposed to do until then?"

"The man has a small house. It was his sister's; she does not live there anymore. He offers it for your use tonight." Charanjit looked over his shoulder, and Benton saw a small white-haired man standing in the shade, watching them. "His wife will make dinner for you, for a few rupees more."

Benton smiled and spread his hands, helpless. "No problem."

ఌ ఌ ఌ

The "small house" was a single-room shack, thatched with mud and straw, which stood in the shade of a great tamarind tree. The mechanic's compound, with its wilting garden and outbuildings surrounding the main house, stood across a dry plain of pebbles twenty yards away.

Benton ducked his head under the lintel and stepped into the room. It was bare, except for the bed: an old twin-sized iron frame and a mattress covered with rust stains. The windows were simple square holes in the north and south walls; the door was an empty rectangle facing the east. The smooth stone floor was strewn with tiny dry leaves and the red dust of the plain.

He set down his suitcase in the corner and turned to the mechanic's wife. "It is good," he said in Marathi, trying to be polite. "Thank you."

She was a thick-waisted matron in her fifties, her hair wound into a sloppy knot the color of iron; her brows were thick and black, joined into a single line over the eyes. The mother of six children, her youngest son was still young enough to cling. He wore nothing but a dhoti in the heat; his sorrowful eyes and thin brown limbs gave him the look of a baby monkey.

Seeing that her guest gave the accommodations his approval, she nodded; she did not return his smile, but seemed to relax. "I will send a cloth for your bed, and water. Trusha will come for you when it is time for the meal."

"I regret to say that I cannot come to the house to eat," he said, switching back to Hindi—his Marathi wasn't good enough to communicate a sophisticated thought. "I must stay with my cameras tonight. If a thief were to take these things, I would be unable to work."

She frowned, the thunderous uni-brow descending. "We have had no trouble with thieves here."

"A stranger can sometimes find trouble where a native of the village cannot." He smiled sadly. "I have learned this over the years."

She looked up to meet his eyes, and found a smile that did not falter. Despite herself, the corner of her mouth twitched upward, as if she would smile back. "Jeevan will bring your food to you," she said firmly. As she named the boy, her hand touched his hair; he turned up his chin to look at her, eyes radiant with love, wrapping his arm tighter about the pillar of her thigh.

"Thank you. I am happy to give him a few rupees for his trouble." Benton gave a small bow. He watched her go, her son capering along beside her as her tunic blew in the wind. Then he went to the corner and disentangled his camera bags from his neck, setting them down in the dust beside his battered suitcase.

Alone, he bent his arms and stretched his aching back. He went to the bed and quickly heaved the mattress up, hoping to startle any six- or eight-legged occupants into a panicked scuttle; there was no movement. When the mechanic's daughter came, she found him sitting on the bare mattress, bent over with his elbows on his knees, smoking a cigarette. He looked up at the shuffle of her slippers in the dust and saw her black silhouette in the doorway. She was balancing an aluminum ewer of water on her head and a bundle of blankets on her hip.

He stood as she entered the room. She was a younger version of her mother, perhaps sixteen, with dark brows already knitted over her nose; nonetheless she smiled, as she handed him the jug, and her teeth were lovely and white. When she bent to spread a thin cotton sheet over his mattress, her brilliant persimmon-orange sari pulled tight over the round hillocks of rump and thigh; for a moment he found himself tempted to abuse his host's hospitality.

She seemed to sense his hungry gaze on her body, and spent a few extra moments tucking the blanket. When she straightened and turned to meet his eyes, Benton forced himself to look away—whipping the beast within back into its cage. *Not now.* "Thank you."

She did not speak, but turned and left him alone with the heat. Benton went to lie down on the freshly-made bed, breathing in the house smells which had saturated the smooth, polished strands of cotton. Cooking oil, cumin, sandalwood incense...He closed his eyes, listening to the thirsty wind blow through the dry leaves above. In time, the relentless sound and the hypnotic smell of perfumed smoke had lulled him into fitful, sweating sleep.

ଊ ଊ ଊ

He woke when the wind turned; a cool gust rolled in the door, plucking at his shirt-sleeve. Benton sat up abruptly and threw his legs over the side of the bed. There had been a dream, but it was shattered into unintelligible fragments the moment he opened his eyes; now it vanished in a swirl of inner turmoil, leaving his chest and belly aching with a painful emotion for which he had no name.

His mouth had opened in his sleep, and his tongue was coated with gummy resin. He picked up his jug and drank, swallowing three great gulps of the earth-tasting water; he held the fourth until the tissues of his mouth swelled with the liquid. When his tongue was slippery again, he swallowed what remained, licked his chapped lips and set the jug down.

He stood unsteadily and reached for his cigarettes, wiping away the hot mask of sweat on his face with his shirtsleeve. The room was full of shadows, and the sky outside had gone the bruised color of a blue plum. He went to the doorway; several of his shirt buttons had opened as he slept, and now another gust of wind touched his bare neck and chest, cooling the sweat like a lover's breath. There was a smell of rain in the air.

The monsoon was coming—this time it would not tease and then retreat. He picked up his camera in the last light of day to photograph the clouds that natives called "the army of Indra"—a towering range of rolling thunderheads, black with promise, which swept across the entire eastern horizon. Lightning glinted in the depths of the oncoming storm; Benton let the frames snap through the end of his roll, hoping multiple exposures would give him at least one perfect frame of that scintillating mass.

Thunder thrummed across the plain, still many miles distant. The tamarind tree trembled in anticipation. Benton heard the rattle of a door, and then the quick pit-pat of bare feet across the pebbles; here was Jeevan, carrying two big bowls. Benton brushed the cherry from his cigarette on the doorframe and pocketed the unlit remainder, smiling as the shy boy sidled up to his hut. He reached into his pocket, taking out two coins, and traded them for a bowl of saffron rice—pretending not to notice the distinctly child-sized bite missing from the edge of the scoop on top. Jeevan handed him a second bowl, filled with fragrant curry; three warm loaves of *bhakari* bread served as a lid. Then the little monkey skipped away back to his mother's house. He held his coins in two cupped hands, like a captured cricket, and shook them next to his ear to hear them jingle.

Benton sat down cross-legged in the doorway, removing an old stainless steel spoon from his suitcase. The woman had gone out of her way to earn the ten rupees he was paying for this meal. Her curry was rich, a pool of spicy oil and chunks of tender goat's meat—so good that he saved the last oily cake of flat bread for the end, to mop every last speck from the bowl. The rice was sweet and sticky, heavily laden with golden raisins, minced mango and crumbled almonds. He decided to save most of it for the morning, laying a pair of heavy hard-bound notebooks across the top of the bowl to keep the bugs out.

After a quick visit to the family outhouse in the garden, Benton returned to the empty little shack. Darkness had come. He sat down and took off his shoes, balling up a sock to stuff into each one before he put them down beside the bed. He relaxed, stretched out to luxuriate in his full belly and a cool breeze, smoked the remainder of his cigarette in the dark and then crushed out the stub against the wall. The ambient temperature of the room had dropped several degrees, and for the first time in days he rolled himself up in a thin blanket to sleep. He drifted off painlessly, listening to the lullaby of distant thunder and the croon of an east wind.

☙ ☙ ☙

He woke in the pitch black, wind whipping over him in cool velvety billows. Benton sat bolt upright in bed, blinking against the darkness. His heart was beating fast and hard; the air was heavy with the weight of another human presence, and he strained to pinpoint its location.

All he could hear was the thin whisper of rain, hissing across the gravel outside, sifting through the canopy of the tall tree, trickling and dripping from the roof, the windowsills, the leaves. Lightning flared somewhere in the night, casting a split second of harsh illumination—in that light he saw her standing in the doorway, muffled and hooded in her sari.

"Who is there?" he demanded in Hindi. Brain still fuzzy from sleep, he fumbled for a name from the mechanic's household. "Trusha?"

Her low, musical laugh trickled across the space between them. "Not Trusha."

Thunder suddenly split the night with its roar; as if in answer, a fierce new sheet of rain swept across the village. Benton reached hastily into his shirt pocket and removed his lighter. He held it aloft and flicked it alight.

"What do you want?"

It took a moment for his eyes to adjust. She was still standing in the doorway. Her body was wound in a royal blue sari, embroidered with glistening silver thread; the fabric had soaked up so much rain that it now appeared almost black. Her face was wrapped in a twist of the silk which served as both headscarf and veil. As he watched, she reached up with bare arms and unwound it, letting the sodden tail of fabric fall behind her shoulder.

His heart tumbled out of rhythm. Her face was a round soft circle the color of honey, framed with a coil of jet-black hair. Black brows arched like wings over huge, luminous eyes; no caste mark was painted between them. Her nose was straight, nostrils sweeping to the side in delicate curls. Her mouth was broad, sensuous, lips lush and full and dark. To reveal such a face was like drawing a sword. Benton had never felt quite so defenseless, sitting alone in a bed.

She smiled slowly, and in her eyes he read the wicked intent of every woman since Eve. "What do you want?" she said, touching her dark lip with a rosy tongue. She had simply repeated his words, but her softly teasing tone made him shiver.

She turned her head to the side, one hand slipping to her nape, and suddenly her hair was free, spooling down her slim neck. She closed her eyes, thick black lashes stark against her pale cheek, and teased the rope with her fingers; the strands separated into fat, looping serpents.

The beast inside him answered with a roar. He sat stock still, breathing deeply, as her delicate hand went to the brooch just below her left shoulder. If she released that pin, the sari would fall; she cocked her head at him coquettishly, her eyes asking the question—"Should I?" For a moment he let his eyes drop from her lascivious face to the soft abundance of breast and belly below. The wet folds of her dress muffled her curves, but even at this distance he could see her nipples standing hard beneath the silk.

He raised the lighter's flame higher and made a beckoning gesture with his free hand.

She come to him slowly, sinuous hips shifting as she moved with the rhythm of the whipping rain. He looked down at her little feet, and the heavy, sodden hem leaving a dark trail across the floor; it was odd that she wore no rings on her toes or fingers. Looking up, he found her standing beside the bed; he inhaled sharply as she bent to kiss him, her eyes half-closed. Her lips were cool and soft. The smell of rain was powerful. Her hand touched his, and he suddenly realized that the burning hot metal of the lighter was scorching his thumb; the flame winked out as it fell from his hand, clattering to the floor.

Her mouth parted over his, the tip of her tongue touching him softly; her wet hand found his hot neck and trailed down the open shirt-front to the matted hair of his chest. Hungrily he reached down, finding his own buttons easily in the dark. With both hands she pressed the shirt back over his shoulders; she broke her kiss as she pushed it down his arms and then tossed it away. He gasped with pleasure as her lips found his shoulder and neck; already her mouth was growing warmer.

With her palms she forced him back onto his elbows; there was something ferocious about the way she pulled the blanket away from his legs, twisting her way down his belly with open-mouthed kisses. He found himself hissing each breath between clenched teeth, lips drawn back into a half-snarl. He put his hand to the back of her head, holding her for a moment as her tongue trailed along the border of his waistband and her fingers worked busily at the zipper of his pants. Already he was rampant and aching for her, thinking of the moment when those sweet lips would engulf him; he could feel himself drip in anticipation of that pleasure.

"Wait." He tried to stop her, seized by sudden doubt. A whirlwind of fears went through him, not least the length of time that had passed since he had a proper shower.

"I cannot. I must taste you, *ishta*." Despite himself he shook at the sound of her husky voice; he could hear the need in it, as stark and urgent as his own. Her lips found him, even through the barrier of thin cotton, and hungrily kissed the length of him. His hand clenched involuntarily in her hair, and he lifted his hips for her as she skinned off his jeans.

She cooed gently, and her cheek rubbed against his erection in a slow, sensual circle. She kissed his thigh, worried his skin softly with her little teeth; he made a sound low in his chest as she traced the shape of his member through his briefs with her fingertips, cupped his testicles in the curve of her palm.

"Come here." He drew her up, wrapped his arms around her waist as she knelt astride his body. The brooch of her sari made a musical sound as it skittered across the floor, and suddenly the cold wet silk was slithering down, falling away from her skin; she unbound the tie at her hip and drew the whole rasping cocoon of fabric away, freeing herself.

Benton pressed his face into her belly, hoping to nuzzle deep into a soft mound, but he found the curve beneath his lips as hard as a drum. Marveling at it, his fingertips passed over the taut bowl, sweeping downward to the sensuous tickle of the hair on her *mons*, up again to the heavy fruit of her breasts and the tightly wrinkled pebbles of nipple.

She sighed, her nails trailing over his back. Finding softness, he buried his face between her breasts, kissing and mouthing the cool, yielding flesh. He took them in his hands, growling at the weight, and brushed one tender aureola with the bristles of his unshaven cheek. She hissed, nails running up the nape of his neck with a deeper bite, and he grinned in the dark.

When he took her nipple into his mouth, he could taste the new flavor—a creamy sweetness on the tongue. She gripped him tighter with a cry, is if to press him further into her flesh, and obligingly he increased the pressure of the suction—then made a sharp, muffled exclamation of surprise in the back of his throat, as his mouth filled with hot liquid.

She moaned with pleasure. Despite himself, he drew back. He held the mouthful for a moment, rolling it over his tongue—a thin warm syrup, like oil and honey mixed together. She made another pleading sound, a high-pitched sigh, and the tide of his blood rose high enough to howl in his ears; he had never made love to a pregnant woman before, but the thought was surprisingly arousing. He took as much of her breast into his mouth as he could, sucking hard and swallowing greedily—as if he were the child that she would bear.

She pressed him down onto his back and squatted above him to mount, her heels digging deeply into the mattress. He caressed her round belly with his hands as she reached behind to grasp his member, teasing herself with its heavy head, greasing him with slippery dew. Here at last her skin was warm, even feverishly hot; he could feel the fierce heat of the swollen folds as he passed back and forth between them, and finally slid home into the depths of her body.

The storm was directly overhead now, and the lightning was nearly continuous, lashing back and forth through the violent sky. By the flickering light Benton reached up to her pale breasts, round as two moons above him. As she slowly began to ride, he kneaded them, harder as he felt the answering flood that rushed down his length inside her, hard enough to make her lips part with a sharp cry of pleasure that could be heard above the cannon's roar of thunder.

Her breasts ran with excitement as he squeezed them, sending a slow flow of oil down over the backs of his hands, his wrists, his forearms. By the time she had finished, there were twin pools in the hollow of each collarbone, on his chest… and when she collapsed into his waiting arms, she laughed and lapped them up.

೧೩ ೧೩ ೧೩

The rain and the love-making did not stop for the remainder of the night. Despite her condition, the woman was an avid, agile lover, and her playful hands and tongue resurrected him more times than he would have thought possible on such short acquaintance.

At last the storm seemed to mellow, the lightning and thunder giving way to a steady downpour. Benton cradled her in his arms, caressing her silky body in the dark, letting the endless glossy length of her hair glide between his fingers. She sighed, nestling beneath his arm in the narrow bed, her pregnant belly pressed into his hip, her soft lips open against his skin.

"What is your name?" He spoke softly. For hours he had been afraid to speak.

"You may call me *Neha*." He felt her smile in the dark.

He gave her nipple one last playful tweak. "Why did you come to me, Neha?"

She yawned. "Because you were thirsty, *ishta*."

"Where do you come from? Do you live in this town?"

She let her nails glide over his chest and belly gently. "Ask Charanjit in the morning," she suggested playfully.

He smiled; his driver knew him too well. Surprising that he would have chosen a pregnant prostitute, of course—but perhaps she was the only one in the village.

"You are beautiful, Neha."

"You please me, Joseph," she replied. "Now sleep."

Monsoon

When he woke, the dawn light had suffused the clouds with silver-gray. He sat up in bed just in time to see her hesitate in the doorway, the folds of her sari gathered carelessly about her; she had not bothered to tie it, but simply held it to her breasts like a bed sheet.

For a moment he just looked at her: the sensuous raven's-wing tumble of hair, the cello curve of her bare back, the sweet dimples where her broad hips flared from a slim waist. She looked back over her shoulder, half-turning to smile.

"Let me take your picture." He jumped naked out of bed at the impulse, went to his camera bag, pulled out the Nikon—he knew it was loaded. "I want to remember you."

Her eyes sparkled with humor. "You will, *ishta*." She made a careless, exquisite gesture with her hand, twirling it like a dancer. "But you may take your picture nonetheless."

He opened the lens cap, adjusted the focus, squatted on his heels to put her into the frame—letting his years of experience guide him as he adjusted the aperture for the light. He clicked the shutter again and again. With each moment, she seemed more perfectly beautiful.

At last the roll was finished, and without a word she turned and walked away in the rain, disappearing almost instantly into the mist.

Benton returned to his bed and slept again, satiated for the first time in weeks.

ଓ ଓ ଓ

Charanjit came to the door as Benton sat eating the last of his sweet rice, sometime around noon. "We are ready to roll, my friend." His clothes were soaked from head to toe and his puttees were spattered with mud, but his smile was cheerful. "The radiator is fixed."

"Good." Benton smiled back. "I owe you for last night."

Charanjit cocked his head. "It is nothing. Only a trip to Darwha—you have already paid for the radiator."

Benton chuckled. "No, not that. I was talking about the woman. You'll have to tell me what I owe you—whatever you paid, it was not enough. She was very fine."

Charanjit frowned. "What woman, Joseph? I did not pay for a woman." He looked over his shoulder nervously, at the mechanic's house. "Perhaps we must leave very fast, yes?"

"She said that you knew her. I assumed you had paid her to come to me." Benton paused, taking another bite of rice. "Perhaps she was a friend of yours?"

Charanjit shook his head. "I do not know anyone in this village, Joseph. Of this I am sure."

Benton let the spoon drop into the bowl, annoyed. "When I asked her who she was, she said 'Ask Charanjit in the morning'. You must know her from *somewhere*, for godsakes."

The driver's eyes narrowed. "Tell me about this woman."

Benton paused, a warm flush rising up his chest. For some reason he suddenly felt shy, embarrassed—reluctant to say more. It was nonsense. Charanjit knew him and had seen him do things far worse.

"She was...beautiful." He smiled. "Amazingly beautiful. Black hair, black eyes—her skin was light, but she had no caste mark. Wearing a blue sari embroidered with silver thread...." Seeing no flicker of recognition in Charanjit's eyes, he coughed and added, "About six months pregnant, I would say..."

The driver shrugged helplessly. "Did she tell you her name—?"

Benton hesitated. "She said I could call her *Neha*." A chill crept over his arms, and when he looked down he could see the hair stood on end. "She knew your name, Charanjit. And mine. I don't believe *Neha* was really her name, come to think of it."

Charanjit looked grave. "It is common enough. *Neha* is 'love', in Hindi, or 'rain'—we use the same word for both. A good name for a girl."

Benton fell silent, looking down into his empty bowl. "So you didn't pay her, then."

"No, my friend."

"And you don't know her."

Charanjit silently shook his head, and Benton glanced over at the pile of his camera bags in the corner. They didn't look as if they had been disturbed, but he sighed nonetheless. "Best to see if she took anything, then." Even speaking the words made his chest feel hollow.

The driver stepped over the threshold, tracking red mud onto the floor, and began to pace about awkwardly as Benton squatted to search his baggage. Suddenly, he bent and picked something up from the floor. "What is this?"

Benton glanced over. Charanjit held a glittering object between his fingers. "I don't know. Probably the pin that held her sari."

The driver turned it over in his fingers, musing. "Most unusual. In the shape of the *vajra*. Solid silver, I believe...and this stone might be a sapphire."

Benton frowned. "Let me see that."

Charanjit dropped it into his hand—and seemed curiously glad to be rid of it. Benton held the brooch up, turning it in the light. It was heavier than it looked, shaped like a double-headed Hindu lightning bolt—the blue gem in the center was nearly the size of a quarter.

He whistled. "She'll be wanting this back, that's for certain. It looks valuable."

Charanjit had backed away; when Benton looked up, the driver was strangely pale. "I do not believe you will see her again, my friend." He glanced anxiously out through the doorway. "It is a gift, I think. You should put it away before her husband sees it."

Benton raised his eyebrows. "If you say so." He put the brooch into the pocket of his jeans. "You think she was rich, then? The wife of someone powerful?"

"I think he might be more powerful than you imagine." Charanjit shivered. "I have heard stories of such things before. Come, my friend—let us leave this place. You said you wanted tigers, and we have many miles to go to Chikhaldara."

Benton shrugged. It took only a few minutes to look through all his equipment—entirely unmolested, so far as he could tell. He hiked through the muddy village to the Jeep. The rain had never abated, and it continued now in a steady, gentle shower that might not stop for days or weeks.

As the two men returned to the main road, Benton looked back at the village. The children were out, running together in the rain, laughing and splashing; the earth had already soaked up as much water as it could hold in the night, and now the streets were flowing rivers of mud.

As they drove through the countryside, he stopped the Jeep occasionally to take pictures of the rain's passage. He had seen the end of the dry season before, but this time it struck him with particular force. He wanted to capture the sense of relief, the weight that lifted when the heat was vanquished. Everywhere he turned his lens, there was a man or a beast that stooped at last to drink, eyes closed in bliss. For the first time it occurred to him: *the rain is a gift.*

CB CB CB

Within a few weeks, he had put Neha out of his thoughts; hunting tigers with an arsenal of 35 millimeter cameras took all his attention. It was only when he returned home the next month that he found her silver clasp again, carelessly thrown into a bag with the countless rolls of film he had shot on the trip.

He smiled slightly, closing his eyes. For a vivid moment he could feel her cool flesh against his skin, smell the rain in her hair—taste the warm, ecstatic juices on his tongue. He sorted through the little black film containers to find the one marked "NF6-2": Nikon F6, second roll. He always pre-marked the film canisters before he left home; it made various sequences easier to find.

There was only one subject on this roll. He grinned, tossed it up and caught it in the air boyishly. Yes, this one should definitely be developed first; Neha was by far the most beautiful thing he had seen in India.

When the film was finally dry, he unclipped the long strip from the clothesline and held it up to the light. He frowned immediately as he scanned the repeated image—definitely something wrong there.

There was a cold, queasy tickle in his stomach, but the photographer remained methodical in his work. He laid out the contact sheet: as the white page passed from one bath of chemicals to the next, his heart rate steadily increased. He couldn't wait for the image in the last bath to sharpen completely; he whipped it out of the tub, scanning the images in the blood-red light of the darkroom.

No. Impossible.

In the end he had to make prints of every negative to be absolutely sure. For some reason he kept telling himself that in one of the thirty-six shots he had taken, the woman would still be there: standing in the doorway, looking back over her bare brown shoulder. Those huge, shimmering, merciful eyes…the smile of a satisfied lover on her lips.

But no matter how many prints he made, the image remained the same. The empty rectangle of gray light—the dark earthen wall enclosing it like the borders of a grave. No matter what he did, the doorway was empty.

There was nothing there but the monsoon.

Severity

I am severe
as the desert is,
the sand and rock
in the dry rainshadow
of the mountains.

I have no need
no understanding
of heavy rains;
I come from stony soil,
from little love
and great solitude.

If I give away nothing
that will boil away in the sun,
If I prick and burn,
If I needle you,
If I am not easy to grasp,
remember:

A cactus can grow tall
and even blossom
If it learns to be a cactus.

Don't curse my thorns.
Be glad instead.
Knock a hole in me
with your hoof
with your horn
Cut deep
and refresh yourself...

Arinn Dembo

When you reach the mountains,
indulge your love
of weeping willows.
For now, survive.

Drink from my green heart.

Sisterhood of the Skin

Jones cut a silkie out of the net today; I came up from the hold to find him trying to kill it on deck with a length of pipe. The rest of the swing shift stood around him, giving him a wide berth. Their eyes were hollow and black in the rain. No one wanted to be too near him. He made a broken, high-pitched sound as he struck, squeals of rage wringing out of him in bursts—as if it were him being beaten.

It looked like a female. It made no sound, ribs already broken over vital organs but nowhere near death. That flesh is too tough, flexible, packed thick onto bones like rock. The breasts were swollen. It may have been nursing a calf, down there somewhere in the black water. The golden pelt was spattered with blood, so red and dark that it seemed almost purple. It's mammalian blood, based on iron but thick as gravy; the veins in those sleek, supple bodies are like drain pipes.

For just a second its eyes caught mine. I drew my gun and shot it, erasing the eyes, the winged nostrils, the lion's mouth, the misery. Its face was too much like a woman's. Too much like my own.

Jones looked up at me, frozen in his simian squat with the bloody pipe still in his hand. He was beyond speech. I had an endless moment to hold the targeting beam on the center of his chest and wonder if it wouldn't be best to kill him, drop him over the side and try to cut our losses. His eyes were clear, blue, and utterly vacant—a berserker.

In the end it was simply the fact that I wanted to kill him that decided me against it. I let the barrel of my pistol twitch toward his weapon. He caught the gesture, looked down stupidly at the bent pipe in his hand, and relaxed his grip for long enough to let it slip out of his fingers and fall to the rusting deckplate with a clatter. He lowered his head and wiped at his mouth, like a man wakened from a nightmare; one of the men kicked the pipe away, another touched his shoulder. I holstered the gun. Jones the Elder was back, for what it was worth.

"Let's get this operation back on line before the Captain notices, shall we? You—Gallegos, is it? Get the rest of your crew together and get that thing down to the lab for me. Don't drag it, either. I don't want blood on those stairs." I looked at Jones. What to do with him? He was moving slowly, stiff and numb, to pick up his gear. "Jones, good work. That's a thousand dollar bounty on the silkie, plus the time and a half. You better clock out and spend some time in the hold, or we won't be able to afford the bill we're running up on you."

He rubbed the stiff white bristles at the top of his head with his palm and then nodded, once, in my direction. I watched him go below, his arms swinging dead from the shoulder sockets, like a marionette with half its strings cut.

The sea rolled under the bowsprit far below, boiling away from the prow like surf smashing against the base of a cliff. I went to the rail to smoke a naval cigarette, furtively biting the end to light it. They're supposed to be pinched alight with your fingernails, but the sparking fluid they dip the paper in is mildly hallucinogenic, much more potent than stale tobacco. A lot of the men don't bother smoking them at all, just sit around sucking the ends, pleasantly stoned on the spark.

On the horizon I saw a silkie leap. Perhaps it was a male. It's difficult to say yet whether there are such things as silkie males. I've had only two specimens on the table so far, the one I shot today and the other that drowned in our deep net, which must been a calf. There were hints in the immature physiology which are echoed in the adult. It may be that all the silkies are basically hermaphroditic. It's only because of their faces and mammaries that they seem female to us. I looked out over the rain-ragged swells and saw it clear the waves completely, a thick golden arc far out over the green-black sea.

It leaped over and over, until it became exhausting to watch. That fabulous strength.

☙ ☙ ☙

She was too big to fit easily on the operating table. As the men shoved and dragged the great golden corpse this way and that, trying to get it on the slab, I had to think of Wayland Jones—Jones the Younger—or rather, the pitiful remnant which I had examined a few weeks ago; there was nothing left of him but his arm.

I've drawn my pistol twice on this voyage. I had to force Benito "Bunny" Vicarro to shinny out to the end of the bowsprit at gunpoint in order to recover that arm; it was frozen to a steel safety rung, and the fingers had to be pried off with a knife. Vicarro cried through the whole operation. I'm sure he thought it was vengeance for getting the Jones boy killed. Not true: he was the natural choice. The man is as graceful as a gibbon.

Wayland Jones came out on this trip with his father. He'd never been fishing "off the rock" before—that is, off his home planet. I don't remember much about him, sadly. He shared his father's terse, powerful genetic code: thick body, heavy arms, bandy legs, mastiff's jaw. A product of unusually high gravity. He had all of his father's virtues as a seaman and a fisherman, without the temper so far as I could tell. He also had dark, curly hair—a gift from his mother, whoever she may have been.

Hazing is the rule on a first voyage. I'm sure that Jones, Vicarro and Templeton thought nothing of making the poor kid crawl out on the bowsprit to knock off the icicles forming on the gigantic pole—without telling him that it would all melt off in seconds if we sent out a burst transmission; the Albatross can generate several gigawatts of power. Jones Jr. gamely hugged the pylon and humped his way slowly out over the sea: a hammer in one hand, finding his grip with the other, while the freezing spindle plunged sickeningly over the waves.

I was in the foc's'le tower, looking over our satellite photographs of the area, trying to locate the next school of "fish" in the feeding grounds. I saw Jones Jr. when I happened to look out the window; he had already gone quite a distance from the main body of the ship. He was hugging the transmitter and flailing at the underside with a mallet.

I went to the com to tell him to get the hell off before he got himself killed. The waters of this planet are full of fluorocarbons; they freeze at an extremely low temperature, and even in full gear a man is not likely to survive for more than five minutes overboard—also, we were making at least thirty knots, and he might very well have been sucked into the static envelope and crushed before we could pull him out of the drink.

He seemed to see something in the sea beneath him. He lost a toe grip and he was suddenly hanging by one hand from the bowsprit, dangling over the swirling water; on deck his father and shipmates jumped up and down in silent glee—a tribe of victorious chimpanzees dressed in men's clothes. From the foc's'le I saw what they could not: the pale shape, skimming *fast* just under the translucent green surface. I reached for the controls of the forward ice cannon, but I was much too slow.

The silkie reared from the water like a golden-bronze geyser. In the flood lights the men on deck saw it at last, all four meters of the enormous flexing body completely clear of the chop, dancing backward on its tail...reaching for young Jones with long, slender flippers open like arms. The monitors did not catch his shriek of terror when its body struck him, twirling him around on the pivot of his wrist like a pig squealing over the slaughtering trough; in the tapes you only see his open mouth, gaping wide for a soundless scream.

It caught him, one limb over his shoulder and the other around his chest—it hugged him like a girl leaping onto her lover's back, wanting him to carry her—and sank its muzzle into the muscle layered over his collar bone, tusks shearing through tendons, shattering bones. For a moment, his arm heroically supported them both. The silkie's weight was so tremendous that the arm ripped free at the shoulder before his grip could weaken enough to drop him into the sea.

The elder Jones lunged over and over against the men restraining him, howling, clawing at them; he would have gone overboard if they had lost hold of him. Several cubic centimeters of thorazine were required before he could be quieted. It was not the best drug for the purpose, but it was handy in the psych cabinet and I had no time for subtleties; it took six men just to throw him down the stairs into the lab.

I would have liked to try and trace the silkie: not possible. Jones distracted me for a few crucial minutes, and this ocean smothers our maximum sonar output within three hundred meters of the ship—our loudest shout is lost in the roar of the seismic tide. The Captain belayed my order to submerge the Albatross and search. The silkie took her prey unseen and unhindered down into the dark.

ೞ ೞ ೞ

I finished my autopsy of the creature sometime during the first shift this morning, rinsed off my isolation gear under a spray of green antiseptic in the lab and then hiked wearily up the narrow iron staircase to my quarters. The suit had to stripped off piece by piece and dropped into the autoclave, and my skin scrubbed until my body stings all over and I'm half-boiled. Still, I feel a fever coming on; my teeth are already starting to chatter with anaphylactic chills; there must be elements in that thick blood which can penetrate my skin. The passage of my throat is narrowing. Feels as if the air is thickening somehow, becoming more difficult to breathe. My body is attacking itself—and good riddance.

I never have wanted this body. I've applied a dozen times for improvements, been denied every time. Even the simplest things, like full spectrum eyes. Some of the crew have them. Or a simple immune enhancement. If I had one I wouldn't be suffering like this now. My False Counselor always relays the same message:

"We've found that implants are inadvisable in cases like yours, Ms. Tso. These improvements are poorly suited to a personality motivated by feelings of inadequacy. I can't recommend the procedure, based on your record." One doesn't have the luxury of hating that placid, smoothly animated face; the computer is perfect, it cannot err. The Counselor program is so realistic that it took me six months to realize that I wasn't actually seeing a human therapist—a good one. It provided all the encouraging noises and probing questions I'd come to expect from a psychologist. "If you need to talk, you know I'm always available."

The hate belongs at home. If you have to hate anything, hate this weak, flabby, fallible shell; hate the personal failings that have trapped you inside it.

At any rate, I can't sleep with my breath being squeezed away; might as well record my impressions of the silkie for future reflection.

This was apparently the one that got Jones. I found a naval wristwatch and three old copper coins on a chain—a good luck charm!—in its digestive tract. These were in one of several secondary stomachs which surround the much larger primary digestive cavity. I can't determine the purpose for these subsidiary organs; at first I thought I might have stumbled on a second reproductive system—those nine egg-plant shaped stomachs were beribboned with blood vessels and glands, much more suggestive of a uterus than any kind of gastric organ. The presence of Jones' personal affects seems to suggest that they serve to store indigestible items until they can be expelled. I have recovered stones from two of the other stomachs; these are coated with a thick, nacreous fluid. Do the silkies form pearls in order to protect the delicate alimentary canal?

The intestines are fascinating and also very unusual; the walls are covered with filaments, which seem to serve a double purpose: they absorb nutrients from digested food (an ungodly amount of "fish" in the silkie's gut, in various stages of digestion; they must feed several hours a day) and they also seem to "feel" the food, palpate it as it passes through the digestive tract. The filaments are loaded with nervous tissue, and the area is incredibly blood rich and sensitive. (NOTE: An ingestible poison may be the best way to deal with these animals, should they become a serious problem.) The spinal cord is only inches away from the gut; the nerve fibers are dense in the area, a thick springy webbing which I was not able to examine in fine detail.

The error I made in destroying its skull when I killed it may have been a blessing in the end. If there had been a brain intact, I might have spent all my available time examining it, trying to determine its potential intelligence—I might not have gotten to the rest of the body at all. The Company xenobiologists would have plumbed the secrets of its carcass in a lab many light years from here.

I'll send a full report to the Captain, along with my recommendations: I don't think the elder Jones needs to be informed of the silkie's payload. The man seems to be teetering dangerously; I'd hate to think that the revelation would destabilize him further. I'd like to keep him functioning for another three weeks, until we can bring the load in. It's the biggest haul on this circuit, our first virgin ocean. Even after three hundred years (subjective time) to restock themselves, the fish parks can't yield the bounty that we're taking now; four cubic miles of fish in a net, two nets full to brimming every week...A world never yields its maidenhead twice.

☙ ☙ ☙

Woke up after the first shift when my fever broke. Still weak. I can't face the Captain; I've logged my report.

I dreamed of my father. I saw his face, the two paradoxical halves of it; I was sitting on his lap, very small—small enough again to touch his hard cheek, to polish his glowing golden eye, and feel its heat through a chamois cloth. His flesh eye never seemed as human or real as the other; it was nothing but a sad brown relic. Just so, his flesh hand never seemed as gentle or skilled as the cybernetic one.

My mother was in the dream as well.

My father came to us in the *hogan*. He walked in without speaking and sat heavily at the table. The chair croaked under him like an old woman carrying a load of firewood. He opened his battered pectoral plate—his chest split open like a *piñata*. Candy showered onto the tabletop. He looked down on me, his daughter, and smiled.

Mother stood by the stove, wrapped in blankets and ropes of silver. She was a wealthy woman who married outside her own tribe; my father was a half-breed Lakota before he became a god of destruction. She poured out a bowl of blue corn mush and set it down in front of him, her lips pressed tight. He looked down at the bowl and suddenly went still, shut off like an automaton.

It was too much for her. She went to the corner and bent to pick up his portable generator, because he didn't have a saddle and she had to throw something out the door. This is what women on the reservation must do to declare a divorce. He slept, sitting upright at the table with his head bent slightly, as if he were studying his scorched armor. His chest did not move as he breathed.

She dragged the machine to the door, bent nearly double by its weight, while I sat eating my candies two at a time, heedless of the flavors mishmashed in my mouth, afraid she would take them away from me. My mother grunted, freeing one hand to open the screen door. She threw the generator out into the red dusty yard. It exploded in a shower of sparks as it hit the ground, and my father snapped upright in his chair, his movement so swift and well-oiled that it could never be mistaken for human.

I don't think he even recognized her. She had cut off his power when he was weak and exhausted. She was a threat. He fired two scissoring beams which plunged into her belly and chest, and she burst into a hot, stinging cloud of superheated red steam. Her four limbs were lost in four directions, and I lay on the kitchen floor, burned and crying—her blood was so hot.

He had great difficulty remembering sometimes who the enemy was. I woke one night a few years later to find his golden eye trained on me, sights open. I begged him not to shoot, calling him Poppy the way I did when I was four. He went back to bed, shaking his head slowly from side to side. It took weeks sometimes before the Company repaired the damage to his brain.

They separated us after my "incident". Better for both of us, they said.

ଔ ଔ ଔ

Things on deck look good. I've brought miso to the foc's'le and the mid shift reports a school in the nets. There are men on the winches, easing the deep net into the hold to let the seawater drain. I've assigned a few dozen slimers to a watch on deck and on the sonar. I don't want to lose any more chances at a silkie. The women seem grateful for a break from cleaning fish. The machinery can handle it for a few hours; the humans are really only there to maintain standards of quality.

Fascinating creatures, these silkies. They must be rare, or the probes would have spotted them along with our prey. They wouldn't have sent us here if there were any visible Samoans. Bad policy.

This planet is sometimes very beautiful. If only there were any land, someone would colonize it; the waters are loaded with life. Inuit or Norwegian settlers would do well. I can imagine their hide boats on the water, slipping easily over these beds of vegetation where the Albatross cannot venture—*curachs* and *kayaks* following that trail of twisting green fire which dances on the skin of the sea. They would hunt the silkie as they hunted the orca, with bone-tipped spears.

ଔ ଔ ଔ

Lost another man. Still not sure how. Gunther Jones is being held accountable at the moment.

Sometime during first shift today, the crew went in to gas the drained catch in the hold. Simple enough procedure; we've done it a dozen times. The fish are too strong to be gutted live. They have teeth sharp enough and jaws strong enough to snap off a length of two-inch titanium pipe. However, they are susceptible to ethylene gas, which is generally harmless to the men, once it disperses. It asphyxiates the fish within minutes and dissipates quickly enough that they can be processed and packed without danger of spoilage. The crew goes through the job in about twenty minutes, firing their gas hoses into the net.

They claim that this time, the fish fired back.

I've watched the tapes, I attended the interrogations…the officers scoured the hold with everything but an electron microscope. There was no weapon. No perpetrator. No fish, either. The net was unmoored in the fracas and dropped back into the ocean. Half a million dollars rained back into the soup and swam as fast as fins could carry them to the deepest, blackest crevasse in the sea. It reflects on us, not the cyborg officers; despite their general disinterest in shipboard affairs, the Company holds them to be infallible.

The tapes, as usual, are useless. Nothing but gouts of red light ripping through the sudden torrent of fish, ethylene canisters howling out their contents without hands to control to the flow, men screaming, James Freedman burning. It was obviously a nasty little T-rod that did the job, the sort of laser mining torch that sailors can buy in any port in the system—nastier than most. I've got a man laid out in my lab who's missing most of the left side of his body. Your average black market laser can't generate that kind of power.

It doesn't matter. Jones has gone insane. He must have dropped his weapon into the water after firing it at Freedman—or perhaps, much less likely, after firing at a man standing on the other side of the hold. The walls are polished steel. It's not strictly impossible that they could have reflected the energy, some kind of ricochet effect. Jones was standing one man over from Freedman at the time. This is the current consensus: the beams coming out of the net would be just an illusion caused by darkness, gas, confusion.

No sense can be extracted from Jones at all. After the last frenzied assertion that someone in the net was shooting at him, I put him down. His constitution is such that no tranquilizer will hold for long; it may be more economical to put him back into suspension for the duration of the trip. Of course, the extra time will partially drain his tank, but it's more than possible to transfer him to his son's berth for the journey home. Or Freedman's, for that matter.

We're behind, thanks to this appalling accident. We'll have to bring in another load before we can climb the well and get off this spinning ball of slush, and then take the short way home in order to make it in on schedule. The cargo is already promised to half a dozen hungry worlds. If we don't deliver, I can say goodbye to any chance of leaving this kind of duty; for that matter, I might pull worse. I'm the sci-med on this scow, for what it's worth—an officer, despite the fact that I'm all meat and no metal.

I'll take the obligatory look at Freedman, although I'm sure there isn't anything else to find. I'm getting very tired.

ଔ ଔ ଔ

A man crossed himself before obeying my orders. Such a familiar gesture that I stood gaping at him for a few seconds, while he eyed me sidelong, his eyes long, dark, dubious. The gesture was so pervasive throughout my childhood and youth that seeing it ripped me out of time: Spanish women crossing themselves at my father and me as we ate ice cream in front of the Palace of the Governors. For a moment, I felt what my father must have felt; contempt, indifference, shock. Shame under it all, the nagging shame of one who has surpassed the species in some grotesque way.

There aren't enough places to lay out cadavers in this scabby little kitchenette/laboratory. The silkie occupies the operating table, Freedman's body I've balanced on the open counter by the sink; I only need the one side anyway. Jones is still in the tank, and there shouldn't be any need to lay him out anywhere, if he'll just cooperate. The tank is unwieldy, blocks the door to the lab. Who cares? A crowded little den of science.

Damned glad I managed to get a bead on this silkie when she cleared the water. Of course, I was only being professional. I didn't think I'd hit her, but I knew I wouldn't get another shot at her. That's the second time I've been lucky. It's statistically unrealistic to expect the luck I'll need to get away with this—these investigations of mine are pure indulgence. I should be carving up fish, not hunting mermaids.

She doesn't look much like a silkie now. The flippers have become articulated into five digits, one of which looks distinctly opposable. Coincidence? Impossible. The bones are much more plastic than previously; they actually bend in the middle like green wood. This, in contrast to the first adult Jones brought in; she had bones like granite. The skull is also softened, unknitted; it has to be. *The thing was growing a new face.* I can't imagine how it was happening, but I intend to find out.

ଔ ଔ ଔ

I questioned Jones before he was fully awakened from his deep sleep, still lying half-buried in the shining shock gel of the suspension tank. He stirred feebly as I wiped the cold jelly from his face and peeled away the mask so that he could pull his own oxygen.

"Hello, Gunther. Can you hear me?"

Jones blinked his eyes, slowly and rhythmically. It took me a moment to realize that there must be a film of the jelly coating his corneas; perfectly clear, but it would distort his vision. He opened his mouth, sticky threads stretching between his parted lips, and drew in a rattling breath. I had to lean close to catch his word.

"Dead," he said.

I drew away. He did look dead; worse, hideously resurrected. It was not pleasant to be reminded.

"Am I dead."

His barrel chest seemed to buckle; his shoulders folded together and he sank deeper into the tank. I caught his chin and held his face out of the glistening ooze, not wanting him to drown.

"You're not dead, Gunther." It took some doing, but I kept my grip on his jaw and pulled him further from the tank without actually having to immerse my hands. The suspension medium is perfectly inert and harmless, but very unpleasant to the touch when chilled.

His eyes rolled up in their sockets, leaving nothing but the sickly blue-white sclera staring out of the parted lids, and he began to speak poetry. I believe the first word was a man's name: Norm, or perhaps Norms. The language was old, some guttural, wet Scandinavian tongue.

Jones opened his eyes again; he seemed to see me quite clearly, suddenly, although it was obvious he had not awakened from his psychotic nightmare. "Oh, he's dead, all right. I've seen you. You and your metal men. Dragon's teeth in the water." His lips pulled back from his teeth and he began a mnemonic exercise, one of the simplest, which fishermen are often taught to help control their panic responses when they lie in the suspension tank, waiting to lose consciousness. It was the one which begins:

"I rowed and rowed
until I knowed
there wasn't no more to row,

For I'd come to the place

where the water and waves
turn into the ice and snow..."

"Gunther, did you see Wayland in the net?"

He looked at me, cut off in mid-verse. His mouth moved very slowly into the most malicious smile I have ever seen.

"Was he there, Gunther? Did you see him?"

"—It was all very nice in the mountains of ice..."

He continued to recite it until I turned down the temperature of the suspension and pulled the mask back over his stiffening face. It's useless to try to extract information from the man. His mind is broken and I do not have the professional skills or equipment to mend it.

It's a shame, really. I wanted to know whether he had seen his son bite off James Freedman's arm.

ఠ ఠ ఠ

Apparently my assumption about the last silkie was incorrect. This one was carrying many small bones in her gastric pouches, all of them recognizably human: a few carpal bones, metacarpi, and the terminal digits of a human hand. There almost seem to be too many of them, even given my previous hypothesis that a silkie in the net succeeded in biting off Freedman's arm when he was killed. The bones were coated in a shimmering calcium secretion, which is very similar in nature to a terrestrial mollusk's—spectrographic analysis reveals nothing more unusual than a few skeins of rare mineral, typical of the sediments we dredged from the bottom. It looks very much like mother-of-pearl, although the dominant colors seem to be yellow and red. There must be infinite variation from silkie to silkie.

I could spend days dissecting one of these ladies, but there were important matters at hand. I unceremoniously ripped apart her head, examining the contents with my microscopes and spectrometer. Eventually the tissues were nothing but a blurry, garish soup which I stirred with black pipettes, and I forgot from moment to moment what it was I had been looking for.

The muscles are blood-rich and full of organic compounds, aldehydes, ketones and lactic acid. The silkie must have been using them to fuel its transformation. Opening the skin was remarkably easy; she had lost many layers of dense subcutaneous fat, which made her pelt hang like a loose robe. I had to gather up a fistful of it and pull it almost half a meter away from the solid flesh beneath to make a neat incision.

I cut the savage golden features of the silkie from the tightly wound tendons and pulleys which bound her skull. The face of Wayland Jones was beneath it. The likeness to a human was so startling that the scalpel dropped from my hand and I had to turn away for several moments, holding my own face in my hands—as if I had suddenly thrown back a coffin lid, squatting in the bottom of a rudely opened grave, and found that the occupant was my own brother.

Only the huge, dark eyes had not changed, all pupil but for a rim of muddy brown-black. The orbital ridge was so flexible that I could depress it with my finger, and the upward curve of the cranium was no longer sleek and dynamically sloped as it must have been before. The curving forehead suggested a more developed cerebral cortex, and the bone of the pate was wobbly, almost cartilaginous. I found the new neural growths forming over the old, folded tight just above the structure which is so like a mammalian limbic system. They looked like buds, densely wrinkled and ready to spread a profusion of meninges like the petals of a mum.

                                              ଓ ଓ ଓ

Gallegos finally distracted me from my investigation some time during my fourth consecutive shift in the lab. I did not hear him come in.

"*Madre de Dios.*"

I looked up from the roaring centrifuge and into his wide, staring eyes. I watched, detached, as his face crumpled from shock and disbelieving horror to intense dismay, grief, fear—and a narrow-eyed, shifting look of guilt.

"Way?" He pointed with a finger held close to his own chest, as if afraid the corpse would snap at it.

I stared at him, unable to understand him, for what seemed like several minutes. He offered nothing more, only stood looking at me, obviously waiting for an answer, while the gears in my brain ground slowly, trying to process that one enigmatic syllable. A silent, glazed eternity, two faces as blank as bowls of milk locked in a contest of imbecility. At last I blinked.

"Way...land Jones? No..." I shook my head like a dog, trying to clear the feeling of tiny insects crawling and buzzing in my ears. "No, of course not. Look at the body. It's not Jones—a silkie."

Gallegos crossed himself with one hand and used the other to yank a tarp over the glistening, peeled face of his shipmate. His lips pulled back in a grimace. "It needs to be covered. *A la Verga*...It needs to be *buried*."

Sharp, naked fear washed over my skin. He was right, of course—in a manner of speaking. Gallegos was willing to believe that I'd removed this head from the silkie's stomach, but anyone could have entered the lab during my autopsies and seen the thing. The men are coming in constantly with cuts, colds, fevers. In my delirium, the reaction they would have to this spectacle had never entered my mind. I couldn't let it be seen.

I looked up at Gallegos and let him read my face—the man is quite literate in the language of expression and gesture, for all he signs his name with a leering devil glyph. He looked away, tense and awkward.

"I'll be needing a few men from your crew, sailor. Send them down in an hour." I looked down at the corpse. "I'll be finished by then."

"Aye." He turned and left, rubbing the back of his neck fiercely with one hand as I started up the bone saw.

൪ ൪ ൪

I had a tremendously strong allergic reaction to the silkie's blood. My fever has broken now, but I've been burning for the past several hours. Had strange dreams.

I was holding a tremendous bowl in my arms, filled to the brim with pearls—pearls as big as a naked skull lay half-buried in seed pearls no bigger than drops of honey. A brown woman stood running one languid hand through the bowl, letting the glowing white sand trickle through her long, slender fingers.

She hefted the biggest pearl in two hands and dropped it into a goblet of wine. The cup seemed small, but it grew as big as a vat to receive the pearl. Thick, dark red slopped over the sides and onto her dress; I smelled hot iron and salt. I dropped my bowl. Pearls spilled over my bare feet, and the ground split open; water gushed from the floor, achingly cold. She offered me the edge of her goblet, which she was somehow still able hold. Her hand was gigantic, golden.

"Drink, Beloved." Her voice was thunder. "And you will be transformed." I looked down into the cup, and everything was obliterated but the red reflection of my own face. The red fluid was not wine. It had never been wine. It was silkie's blood, red-violet silkie's blood, with threads of the great pearl in it. A cloud of pale pink boiled up from the bottom of her grail, like milk in a cup of tea. When I wouldn't drink she raised it to her own lips and gulped it down. Blood ran down from the corners of her mouth as she lifted her head.

She put a hand behind my neck and drew me in for a kiss. As our lips met she pushed smaller pearls out of her mouth with her tongue, forcing them into mine.

I swallowed them.

I had other dreams, some even more confusing, some more painful. I dreamed of my "incident" again. It happens often enough when I'm in good health, much more so when I'm sick or over-tired. I've learned how to wake myself up instantly if the dream begins, hauling myself out by the scruff of the neck the moment I see the signs—that light buzzing above the bathroom mirror, my own trembling rust-brown hands in front of my face. This time, I couldn't free myself. I was too weak to achieve true consciousness, and could only lie there, paralyzed, while I watched it all again.

It was the final dose of mnemonic booster that did it, combined with the stimulants I had taken on my third morning without sleep. I was trying to study for my mid-term exams in quantum mechanics. I saw metallic flashes in the corners of my eyes; I became convinced that my eye sockets were made of metal. If I could only peel off this layer of covering flesh, the rubber mask of brown woman-face, I would find my true face beneath it, gleaming. I could recover my birthright, clean away the blood and polish my own eye with a chamois cloth.

The bathroom, the white basin, the razors my Polynesian roommate used to maintain ritual scars on her arms and thighs. I picked one up, holding the little ceramic wafer awkwardly between my fingers, and made an incision at the hairline.

I watched this for the hundredth time, my own hands working to peel away my brow. In reality there was nothing but blood beneath my skin—I was still red, red again, an Indian girl down the marrow of my bones. In my dream, I pulled it all away easily, staring at the steely beauty beneath, my jaw elegantly hinged and socketed. I was delighted, and yet somehow I kept pulling at myself, and the steel came away in pieces, like the peel of a strange metal fruit.

Underneath it all was a silkie's face. She opened her lion's mouth, her soft brown eyes shining. The lips pulled back to reveal her black tusks and purplish gums; she was smiling at me.

"Mother," I said, and at last pulled free of the dream. The Captain's face hovered above mine, gleaming like a steel moon. I looked up into the silver eyes of his hologram, and made some effort to compose my own features.

"Report to the bridge in one hour."

Sisterhood of the Skin

☙ ☙ ☙

The officer's quarters are much larger than those assigned to human crew. There are small stairs which lead down onto an audience platform; a chair had been placed on the platform for me, facing the eight central screens.

"Mister Tso, please sit." The Captain and his staff hung in the rungs and struts all around me, each of them bigger than my cabin. Steam rose from the dripping, trembling hulk of the First Mate—he squatted below me on a dais, all sixteen legs splayed out to dry.

"I would prefer to stand, sir." Gallegos had betrayed me to them, surely. I was prepared for discipline.

"Mister Guon has made several sweeps outside the ship since you submitted your last report on the native predators. He discovered a group of them at the furthest edge of his patrol and recorded their behavior from a distance. We cannot classify the footage. Respectfully request your opinion."

I turned away from them and sat, fighting to control the sudden weakness of relief which swept my body. "It would be my pleasure, sir. Please run at reduced speed."

The curving screen shimmered into a huge curtain of sensuous blue-green, so filled with light that the film could not have been shot more than twenty meters from the surface. Silkies materialized in the softly glowing water, arching their backs. Even at full speed they would have been swimming slowly, gently looping over and over in the water. They swam together, brushing flippers and flukes. I didn't realize until they separated that one of them was partially humaniform—the flippers bent at an unnatural angle when she reached for the others.

I froze. "One of them seems to be injured," I offered. My chest was tight, constricted—I could hardly breathe. It was ghastly to have to lie to them, but I was suddenly certain of what I was about to see, and the need to protect the silkies was uncontrollable. Tears filled my eyes. I've never been in such conflict before. "Perhaps the others are providing aid or comfort."

"Samoan behavior," the Captain said.

"It would be, yes. But this is certainly not conclusive."

"Continue watching."

Other silkies were dimly visible beyond them, pale and dark circling together in the blue gloom. The group separated and swam one after the other, spiraling down into deeper water. The humaniform silkie rolled over and hung nose down in the water, while the others nuzzled at her flukes and the curve of her anterior surface.

"We found these gestures curious."

I knew what was coming. They swam past her one by one and kissed her, rooting in her muzzle for the pearls. I took a deep breath, turned to the council of titans behind me, and lied again—hoping they would mistake the changes in my vital signs as stress and amazement. "These patterns are similar to others I've studied. A high probability of sentience. They must be Samoans, and we've already murdered three of them—God only knows how many will starve." I closed my eyes, shutting out the gigantic screen and its circling forum. "The scoop will have to be aborted."

The Captain and his staff sat in silent communion, exchanging frequencies beyond my hearing. At last he spoke: "I concur. We will climb the well at o-eight hundred hours. Please prepare the crew for flight. All scoop operations will be shut down immediately."

03   03   03

I had very little trouble making my escape.

I loaded Jones myself into a new berth for the trip home. The crew was more than willing to hit the tanks; it was the work of two hours to prepare them for the long sojourn in shock jelly and double check their life support systems. There are only fifty-three humans aboard the Albatross, most of them second or third generation fishermen. Getting into a suspension tank is as easy as pulling a blanket over themselves.

I made my own preparations at dawn. I unbolted one of the portside ice cannons and loaded it onto Launch Sixty-three, *The Red Shoes*, along with my slides, papers and gear. The boat is designed for sampling sea life in a variety of conditions; the generator will continue providing power and heat long after I'm dead of old age. It will still be running when the next ship comes, if it comes—three hundred years from now, or a thousand.

The timing of the drop was delicate. I couldn't give the Captain any time to abort the launch and retrieve me, so I had to eject during the actual lift-off. Wear and tear on the drive mechanism, waste of fuel is worth more than the launch and any ten of the cyborg officers, much less a human one. But I also had to be free of the Albatross and the heavy seas she would cause when she cleared the water.

The Red Shoes has her own static envelope, but nothing would prevent my body being pulped if she tumbled end over end in a tidal wave.

In the end I jettisoned the boat at about t-minus three minutes and opened up the engines full bore for ninety seconds, skimming and leaping through the high chop at about three hundred km/hour. I submerged to fifty meters and gunned the rotors to fight the turbulence; it was milder than expected. The Albatross lifted off on time. My little boat shivered in her inertial bubble and wafted through the sea, trembling under the impact of the violent tides.

ଔ ଔ ଔ

To you, the someday reader of this journal, I offer this explanation of my acts.

All of my life I have been in exile in my own body, forced to live in a stranger's house. Begging, pleading, struggling did no good. I remained a nubbin of helpless flesh surrounded by machines, an insect scurrying among metal giants. To thrive I needed a titanium shell to cover my nakedness. This was not allowed—if anything, because I wanted it too badly.

The silkies are not so judgmental. My hands still feel strangely soft; I put on gloves last night to counter the effects of the silkie's blood on my own physiology. Without the catalytic elements in the pearl as a substrate to carry an appropriate DNA pattern, my own body doesn't know what to do with itself. My carpal bones have softened somewhat in readiness for change; they may firm again by the time I've determined how difficult it will be to achieve my transformation.

The pearls are the primary form of communication among silkies. If they had a song, it couldn't be heard for long distances, and their numbers are small. They developed a language which they could swallow and pass along, a language which prevents them from being out-adapted by any other organism. Any feature which yields an advantage can be absorbed. The story of man's advent is spreading, illustrated among them by blossoming brains and branching flippers.

They seem quite capable to using weapons, given the digits to manipulate them. Freedman was almost certainly shot by the same silkie which ate Jones. She must have been caught in the net with the fish. Armed with the intellect, the opposable thumb, the weapon, perhaps even a memory of how to use it? A formidable opponent. Their bodies are like bio-genetic factories; whatever they can swallow, they can become. The DNA sampling kit I have onboard should be quite interesting to them.

A pod of silkies approached the boat today. I went out on deck to face them. I've killed and dissected them with my own hands, and I knew perfectly well how serious a threat to my personal safety they could be. But my reincarnation can never succeed without them, and I think they know what I'm trying to do. They dove and leaped all around the Red Shoes for over an hour, caressing the hull and peering through the observation ports. At last one of them surged up on the starboard side and caught the rail in her gigantic hands; the ship listed heavily to one side until the envelope was able to compensate for her tremendous weight. She threw one elbow—an articulated elbow!—over the icy rail and held out the other hand to me. Her outstretched fingers were easily long and thick enough to wrap around my waist. In the soft, purplish palm there was a pearl.

Among my own people I was nothing, trapped on the receding shore of evolution. Here, I am the matriarch of a new race. There are always silkies alongside my ship, listening to my voice, to the hum of my engine; they seem to come and go in shifts. I think they've been driving fish into my net. Sometimes they trade pearls with me. If I use the saw, I can easily cut the pearls in half, insert a slip of biomass and return it. I've seen the thickening of a larynx here and there. In my dreams, I hear them singing…and although the sound is strange, I know that every voice is my own.

The day will come when I am able to slide naked into the sea, and swim among my new people as one of their number. I will shed this body and grow strong, golden, a ring of rippling muscle and bones like rock.

They will be prepared when humans come to fish these waters again—men will not find them helpless to defend the schools which feed them, the precious pearls of transformation for which *Homo sapiens* would gladly slaughter them. I give them what they need. When tales of me are passed from mouth to mouth, they will call me *The Changing Woman*. When men and machines are dragged screaming down into the depths, it will be in my name.

I will make them ready, my sisters, my children, my people. Meet us as equals, stranger—or do not venture into the sea.

The Humanist's Prayer

Oh Lord, give me the strength of will
To swallow all the vapid swill
Of those who beat their chests and claim
That they alone speak in Your Name.

Give me the strength to tolerate
The blindness, bigotry and hate
The murder, bullying and rage
They say came from a Bible page.

Oh Lord, when I must hear them preach
The violence they say You teach
Give me the strength to turn my head
And wish them well, instead of dead…

Give me the strength to stay my wrath
To walk upon a higher path
To be superior to fools
Who drag You into public schools.

Oh Lord, I know it gives You pain
To waste a treasure like a brain
Of human compass, human girth
On those who cannot see its worth…

But still, I pray that there's a hope
That even the most dauntless dope
Will someday see the ghastly blight
His "faith" must be, to block Your light.

The fact is, it's a tragic loss
When folks are beaten with a cross.
And nothing makes the angels weep
Like seeing men behave like sheep…

With all their sick, self-righteous ire
And blathering about Hell's fire
They only drive us from You, Lord,
And make us bitter, tired and bored.

Dear God, please make them stay at home
And leave the rest of us alone.
Teach them to love their human kin
Instead of counting every sin!

Of course, I know You'll heed this prayer,
That humanists say everywhere.
In this one irony we trust:
That Jesus Christ was one of us.

We Are Indra

I heard the tale in a great hall, dimly lit and vast. The feeble cyan lights above kept the central aisle dim; the naves and alcoves to either side were illuminated, lush, splendid in detail. The lives and deaths depicted were larger than human, and more savage—larger still because I was so small. I held my father's hand indoors as well as out, and I had not yet learned the trick that older children know, of stepping softly in such solemn places. My footsteps rebounded from the vaulted ceiling and clattered back and forth between the red velvet ropes, as if a dozen invisible girls were hop-walking with us, all in new shoes.

We stopped at the first alcove, and my father lifted me high onto one shoulder so that I could see over the tall grass and into the ancient savannah.

"*Triceratops*. He used to eat grass. See? It's in his mouth."

The monster had several long tassels of grass hanging down on either side of its triangular upper lip. Its shoulders were hunched, head lowered, offering a nasty trio of horns. The eyes were fierce and golden—the eyes of a cat, an eagle, a snake.

"They used to run together in herds. They were like buffalo; see how big those feet are? Think how loud they must have been when they all started running across the plain..."

I looked at the pale splayed feet, the wrinkled hide, the blunt toenails curving down into the dust. They were big feet—each leg was bigger than four of me stitched together. I could make a lot of noise with my own feet; the analogy was clear.

We crossed the hall to the opposite side and looked down into a jungle, standing pools of thick green water and the trunks of black cypress, hairy vines and hanging moss. The light was dull red, and a beast hunched among the ferns with reflective eyes.

"*Stegosaurus*." My father knew all the names. "The plates on his back are for defense, in case a meat-eater should try to bite him."

"Ouch!" I stage-whispered the words to be sure he would hear me. "What about his tail?" I already knew this part; I just wanted to hear it again.

The tail was poised in mid-air, armed with a cluster of spines as long and sharp as javelins. It looked capable, a muscular limb with devastating range. I'm told that an alligator's tail has more kinetic force on impact than a horse's rear hooves—alligator hunters have to tie the tail when they pull the 'gator into the boat, because one blow can snap a grown man's femur clean in two.

"Just one smack in the head," my father said, smiling. "And POW! Dinosaur surprise. Old Stego' might take a bite, too. Those teeth look sharp, don't they?"

The creature somehow seemed more dangerous that triceratops. His legs were stubby, placed for stability rather than speed. His spine was plated with diamond-shaped wafers of stone; he wielded his tail like a wicked mace. There was a sort of microcephalic fury to his aspect, a mindless threat—Stegosaurus was taking all comers, and I was young enough to be afraid of him.

"Did he eat little girls?"

"No, just roots and leaves, mostly. He wouldn't hurt anybody that didn't try and hurt him first."

"Oh."

We continued walking, and I saw them all. *Dimetrodon* and Duckbill. Pterodactyls hung from gleaming wires over *trompe l'oeil* treetops. My father's story was the history of the Earth, and there were giants in the world in those days.

At last the hall ended and opened out into a tremendous chamber with a high ceiling; we came to Golgotha, the place of the skull. The vivid tableaux in the hall leading here paled to insignificance before these, the dreadful bones of the dragon.

It loomed over us, guarding the way; we must pass before Him on one side or the other. The fleshless arms had been drawn up against its breastbone—those arms which seemed obscenely tiny, deformed, held up in an eternal *Oh-my-goodness!* of insanity and chaos.

This was the avatar of a mad god. His jaws gaped in a silent shriek of defiance, full of gleaming black razors. My father did not speak the name; I knew Him. This was the Lizard King, *Naga-Raja*, the Death of Deaths. *Tyrannosaurus Rex*.

At one time, I knew all their names. It was my catechism, and I chanted it dutifully when it was required of me. These were my Apostles. I played with dinosaur miniatures and watched the *Land of the Lost*— it was one of my favourite shows.

Later, the mega fauna lost after the last great Ice Age became a part of my pantheon. In early adolescence I learned the names of my more immediate ancestors: *Cro-Magnon, Neanderthalensis, Homo Erectus, Australopithecus*— even the holy mother, Lucy. Early hominids were placed in context, a product of the natural world like the sabre tooth and the aurochs, the giant crocodile and the woolly mammoth. By extension modern man was also a product of the natural world, and ultimately answerable to the same forces with had brought so many great Races to naught before we rose from all fours.

Thus I came to know my place, as a human, in the grand scheme. My people were inheritors, the descendants of little bastards too tough and too clever to die when the mighty fell.

Now we are the mighty; *Homo sapiens* stands swaggering on the crumbling lip of its own grave, King of Kings, Death of Deaths. Perhaps someday the beetles will crouch under the mounted bones of my father, when Brahma blinks again.

For now I raise my hand toward the sky, and find that it is filled with thunderbolts. I have no need to become a *yogi* to reflect upon these things. My first duty is to live and to love now, to glory in what I will ever know of power and immortality.

I am human, we are Indra, and it is good.

The Other Wife

(an invocation to the goddess Kali)

O Lord, come dance with me
in the light of the burning city.

Pass your hand over my skin
blackened by the choking ash of the pyre.
Beloved, there is no turning back:
Our bridges are all afire.

Behold the wise come to bow before me,
to sip the wine from my cup,
to entwine my wrists and ankles
with living flesh.

I dwell upon the cosmic mountain.
I am the darkness
The terror
The wearer of skulls.

I am the formidable
The frightening
The frenzied
Feminine fire.

Behold the mouth which speaks only truth
dripping with the gore of demons.

I am delight and *daurmanasya*:
Dangerous
Deadly
Drunk
Dancing…

Let me lick the blood from your beard, Beloved.
Weave for me a garland
of fallen flowers.

Give to me the heads of sages
The arms of soldiers
The tongues of poets
The thighs of dancers
The eyes of painters
The loins of sinners
The heart of a saint.

I have come from the field of battle
glutted with the blood of my enemies.

The legions of the mad and the mighty
the wicked and the wise
prophets and princes
follow in my wake.

Lie with me in the cremation ground
in the dust of the dead.
Clutch the double moon
in your terrible hands.

Lie down in *mirtasana*;
I will ride the Pillar of Creation.

Spread your arms
like the crucified Christ.
Bellow your pleasure
Howl your pain.
I will resurrect you
again and again…

The Other Wife

Kiss the lips of my three faces.
Kiss the lids of my three eyes.

Drink the milk, the blood, the ashes
from my laughing mouth.
Entangle yourself in the net
of my terrible deceptions—
the ragged tresses
as dark as death.

Soothe me with sacrifices
and the music of war:

With the tears of widows
With the wails of orphans
The song of jackals
The laughter of crows
The roar of cannons
The breaking of bones.

Adorn me with offerings
Smeared with the nectar of red red blooms
with the glistening pearls
of your desire.

I will teach you the steps of the *tandava* dance.
I am your other wife.
And my time is now.

The Foreordained Rabbit

This is a story which is told to young rabbits on warm summer evenings.

Once upon a time, there was a tribe of rabbits that made camp in a field of tall rye. The wise old rabbits of the tribe forbade the younger rabbits to dig holes and marry; the field was only home for the summer, and the older rabbits knew they would have to move on when the nights grew crisp. The young rabbits, who weren't much for hard work or commitment, were only too happy not to dig holes and get married. And they were willing to humor the older rabbits about "moving-on day" rather than argue about it.

"Who wants to waste time chewing pellets with those gray ears anyway?" they would say, and return to their games.

Among the young rabbits there was one particularly feckless rabbit, a rabbit who was never satisfied to leave well enough alone. He insisted that he knew better than any senile old bag of clover, and he had no intention of letting them tell him what to do. "Why on earth would anyone want to leave the rye field?" he'd say. "It's the best life a buck could ask for. The hawks can't see us; the dogs can't smell us. The weasel and the fox never come here, and the rye is the most beautiful thing in the world."

When he went to the old rabbits, they wagged their heads stubbornly. "We don't remember why we leave the field when the nights grow crisp," they said. "All of us forgot during a winter nap. Nevertheless, it is so; we must all cross the river. There are holes for us on the far bank."

"I like the rye field," the young rabbit declared. "I will not leave it."

"You have damp ears," they said. "Or you would know better than to say anything with such conviction. It smacks of destiny, kitten, and destiny is never a healthy thing for rabbits."

"Destiny, my tail," the young rabbit muttered, once he was out of earshot. He went off for a dust bath and put it out of his mind.

As the weeks passed, however, and he continued to argue that no one should leave the field, the old rabbits began to speak of destiny in more and more ominous tones. The young rabbit's friends took to calling him the Foreordained Rabbit—as a joke, of course, but the laughter grew uneasy as the nights grew cooler. Eventually, it stopped being funny altogether. The summer was drawing to a close, and the Foreordained Rabbit's friends began to avoid him, feeling for some reason that they shouldn't be too near him. Perhaps his destiny was big enough to fall on two, or all.

The Foreordained Rabbit was very unhappy. He knew very well what destiny means for a rabbit: destiny is the hawk's swift stoop and a broken back; destiny is the sudden snap of the fox's jaws, the boneless tumble into death; destiny is the weasel's hypnotic ruby eye. He couldn't blame his friends for staying away if they thought that doom was on his flank, but he couldn't shake the certainty that it was all nonsense.

He took to wandering the rye by himself, listening to the stalks whisper; the field was trying to tell him something, but he could not make out its words. He knew he would never be happy anywhere else; the rye field was the best place in the world. The rye field *was* the world. The good clean smell and the safety of his home reassured him, and he firmed his resolve on these solitary hops. There could be no doubt that he was right, and the old rabbits were wrong.

Perhaps, though, he should go along with his friends and family to the burrows by the river. Perhaps he should keep them company. He would be lonely in the field if he stayed by himself, with no one but beetles and mice to talk to.

Moving-on day arrived, and all of the tribe prepared the leave the rye field. The Foreordained Rabbit danced on his forepaws nervously; he had been against this move for so long that he didn't know how to join the ranks. He hopped along with his fellow rabbits until they came to a ditch at the edge of the field, but as he was about to take his first cautious step into the open, one of the elder rabbits hopped up beside him.

"Are you coming with us, Foreordained Rabbit? You must wait, and let us go ahead. All the tribe is afraid to hop with you."

The Foreordained Rabbit's ears drooped. Without a word he watched the other rabbits go. When he tried to follow, he found himself unable to take the first step. Visions of his destiny, coming to him alone and in the open, paralyzed him. He sat helplessly until the sun set, and finally turned back to sleep in the whispering rye.

He went a little mad in the days that followed, living in the field by himself. He stopped combing his fur; he forgot to eat. Instead he scampered around the field with cockleburs in his tail.

One morning he woke to the sound of great footsteps coming through the rye. The Foreordained Rabbit crouched low; the earth beneath his paws was vibrating.

The Foreordained Rabbit

"Surely now my destiny is here," he thought. The footsteps stopped and he strained to hear what the giant could be doing, over the sigh of the morning breeze.

Swish! was what he heard. And then again: *Swish!*

He stood up on his hind legs cautiously, and then ducked—just in time to avoid being beheaded by the Man's black iron blade. He gave a little scream as the scythe passed whickering over his head.

The rye fell all around him. The footsteps moved on and the Foreordained Rabbit dug frantically into the earth below him, trying to scrape himself a place to hide.

The Man came again; the Foreordained Rabbit huddled in his nest of rye stalks, wall-eyed, pressing his ears flat against his feverish skull. The Man was gathering up the rye in a bundle. *Swish! Swish!* He was cutting the stalks even closer.

Then, at last, He went away.

The Foreordained Rabbit lifted his head slowly. The rye was in ruin, every stalk cut to stubble, heaped upon the ground. But, he reassured himself, it would grow back. It wasn't long until winter, but it was time enough for the rye to grow several inches.

At the edge of the field, the Man put His torch to the ground. The rabbit winced at the smell of destruction, turning his head to escape it; but the Man was there as well, putting the torch to the ground in the west, the north, the south.

The fallen rye burned. The Foreordained Rabbit ran this way and that, trying to escape the smoke, but it was everywhere. Finally he was only a flame dancing among the flames. His whiskers curled and blackened; his tail blazed; his ears became two funnels of fire.

At last he dashed free of the field and tore over the hills, leaving flaming footprints as he ran. "Fire! Fire! Fire!" he screamed, over and over, until he reached the bank of the river. He leaped out and soared, a rabbit and a fireball both at once, and extinguished himself in the dark water below.

Only three rabbits saw him fall. They had been sitting on the far bank to watch the stars.

"Was that a rabbit?" they asked, turning to each other. "Or was it an angel?"

Indigestion

The train rocked and grumbled through the night, lurching from side to side like a drunk staggering down a narrow hallway. The two men, seated diagonally in a four-man compartment, folded their arms and irritably agreed that the tracks between Chicago and D.C. were a disgrace.

"And the food!" Halligan said. He made a fist and thumped his own chest twice for emphasis. "I'm tellin' ya, Amtrak ain't what she used to be. I swear, that chilidog's got a mind of its own. Wants to come back on me something fierce."

His companion smiled and politely refrained from pointing out the obvious: that Mr. Halligan had eaten not one, but three chili dogs in the lounge car an hour ago, and that a man of his age and corpulence should avoid such challenging food after eight p.m.—acid reflux was practically inevitable. Instead, the slim man in the plain gray suit reached into the pocket of his jacket and offered Halligan a roll of antacid tablets. "Would you like one?"

Halligan grunted assent. "Thanks a million, buddy. You're a life saver." He took the roll, tore the wrapper and thumbed out three chalky tablets out into his palm. Then he popped them into his mouth simultaneously and chewed them to dust between his big square teeth.

The man in the gray suit smiled. "Not at all." He looked out the window; mile after sterile mile of industrial hell rolled by, sodium lights winking on the warehouse walls and the stacks and pipes of countless refineries.

"I didn't catch your name, pal," Halligan said, bending forward to return the roll of Tums. The one valiant button of his jacket held fast as the fabric strained over his belly.

The thin man smiled again. He had not offered his name; if he had, Halligan would not have caught it. The fat man had been talking non-stop since he entered the otherwise empty compartment a few hours ago. Oddly, it seemed to make little difference whether the subject of Halligan's soliloquy was politics, race relations, inflation or the state of the country's rail service—somehow all issues centered on him. To Halligan, the world and all its people could only exist in his orbit, like satellites circling an adipose star.

"My name is Banks," the thin man said. "Phillip Banks."

"Well, I'm pleased to meetcha, Phil. Nice to have someone to talk to, this time of night." Halligan took an oversized handkerchief from his pocket and used it to mop the shining blubber of his neck. "Sorry. Damned Amtrak can't keep up the air conditioning in these little rooms, I guess. You get one or two guys in these things, it turns into a steam bath."

Banks nodded and made a gesture toward the casement overhead. "I could open the window, if you like."

"That'd be peachy. Thanks, pal."

Banks stood and pinched the safety clasps at the top of the window, lowered the small rectangular pane to its limit and let in a few inches of the night. With the thin breeze came the stink of the factories and the roar of the train, but these could not be helped. Before he sat down again, he reached over to the door of the berth and pulled down the vinyl shade, which would keep passersby from looking in.

"Good thinkin'," Halligan said. "Last thing we need is more people in here. Let 'em think we're full up and sleeping."

The thin man smiled again as he sat down, adjusting the cuffs of his white linen shirt. "Indeed."

Halligan leaned back in his seat, resting his hands on the dome of his midriff. "So, whaddaya do for a living, Phil? I'm in construction, myself. Probably told ya that at dinner. Got my own company in Philadelphia."

Banks nodded amiably. "Yes. You mentioned that."

"Let me guess." Halligan squinted at the thin man, as if to take his measure: the modest suit, the round wire-rimmed glasses, the clean-shaven face with its permanent expression of mild, friendly astonishment. "Something brainy, I bet. And it pays good. Accountant, maybe?"

Banks shook his head.

"Librarian?"

The thin man's eyes twinkled. "Afraid not."

"Teacher? Something with computers?"

"No, not usually." Banks was still smiling, his hands folded politely in his lap. "Give up?"

Halligan shrugged. "Yeah, I'm stumped." He reached up to pull the knot of his tie, loosening the loop and the collar beneath. "Jeezus, it's hot in here."

Banks looked up casually. "I'm an assassin."

"You?" Halligan had frozen in astonishment, his hand on its way back up to wipe his shining jowls with the handkerchief. Then suddenly, he belched out a roar of laughter.

The thin man's smile did not entirely leave his face. "Yes. Me."

Halligan stopped laughing on a dime. "A hit man?" The fat man burst into laughter again. He laughed so long and so hard that his face flushed brick red;

toward the end he actually started to choke and cough, and it was the coughing that finally throttled the last of his mirth.

Through it all the man in the gray suit did not change his expression—save that an interrogative lift of one eyebrow accompanied his usual smile.

When Halligan recovered himself at last, he shook his heavy head. "Sorry, Phil. Didn't mean to laugh atcha there. It's just…" —a chuckle seemed to bubble up out of his gut again, but he forced it down—"it's just that I've met a few hit men in my time. You?" He chuckled again. "You are *not* the type."

"Not to worry, Mr. Halligan. I understand the confusion. I am certainly not, as you put it, the 'hit man' type." The thin man's nostrils flared slightly as he said the words, as if in distaste. "A 'hit man' is a burly, clumsy goon whose main value to his employer is intimidation. He exists to make certain threats credible: 'Pay up,' the boss will say, 'or Paulie here will break your kneecaps.'" Banks curled down the corners of his mouth in contempt. "He has no independence; he does what he is told to whom he is told, and never questions the reasons why. And if he does manage to kill someone in the line of duty, a 'hit man's' work will be melodramatic, bloody and highly publicized. Even his murders are a form of intimidation—a message, if you will. 'Behave yourself, or this will happen to you.'"

Halligan chuckled again, a bit uneasily. "You got that right, pal. Most people get that message pretty quick, too."

Banks smiled in return. "I'm sure they do. It is a sad fact of life that bullies, amateur and professional, often prosper." He looked down at his nails, as if examining them for dirt. "But if you had listened carefully, Mr. Halligan, you would know I never called myself a 'hit man.'" He raised his chin slightly, pursing his lips. "I am an *assassin*. Quite a different thing."

Halligan snorted and sat back, his face a mask of amused, skeptical disdain. "Yeah? How's that?"

Banks gave an eloquent little shrug—the gesture of a man who has explained something many times, and grown used to being contradicted by the ignorant. "An assassin is an independent businessman—he belongs to no larger organization, be it criminal or political. If he accepts a commission, he does so on his own terms, and for his own reasons. He has no interest in threats or intimidation. He does not deliver 'messages', or commit crimes that anger the authorities and terrorize the general population." The thin man winked. "Quite the contrary, really. An assassin's best work never appears to be a murder at all. When his victim's death is declared an accident, a suicide or a simple heart attack, the assassin is well content."

Halligan made a face and wiped his brow with the handkerchief. In the ensuing silence, he shook his head, took a deep breath, and made a weary, incredulous noise with his mouth—like a horse fluttering its lips. "Pal, you got some strange ideas about guys who bump people off for a living." He sat up straighter, re-arranging his spreading bulk in the seat. "Where'd you get all this guff, anyway? Some book, I bet." He shook his head. "It ain't like that at all."

Banks lifted his eyebrow. "It isn't?"

Halligan pursed his lips and shook his head. "Nah. Like that bit about hit men being big burly guys. That ain't true. Hit men don't have to be big guys, long as they carry a piece."

Banks was amused. "Indeed. As an assassin, I seldom use a firearm."

Halligan rolled his eyes. "Right. And how exactly do you kill guys, Phil? Talk 'em to death?"

The train jigged abruptly to the side, and the light in the compartment flickered and died. The thin man's glasses shone like mirrors in the gloom. "I use various methods," Banks said quietly. "Whatever suits the occasion, really. There are times when one has to take advantage of a sudden opportunity, and use a weapon of convenience. One man stumbles onto the train tracks drunk; another accidentally drowns. A woman alone in her office chokes to death on her take-out lunch." The thin man's teeth flashed with silent laughter. "A grilled chicken burrito can be a frightening thing."

Halligan cleared his throat and shifted in the shadows. "Gotta say, Phil buddy—yer startin' to creep me out."

"Am I?" Again the teeth flashed, slick and pale orange in the light of the industrial wastes outside. "I'm sorry, James. I had no idea you were such a sensitive person."

There was a long silence before Halligan spoke again. "How exactly did you know my first name, Banks?"

Banks paused. "James Francis Halligan," he said lightly. "Age forty-three. Married. Three children. Resident of 1215 Parkview Lane. May I call you James? Everyone else seems to call you 'Jimmy', but 'Jimmy' really doesn't suit a man of your girth, does it? 'Jimmy' is a paperboy's name."

Halligan paused. When he spoke again, his voice had dropped a register. The bluff, blustering buffoon was gone; what spoke from the other side of the alcove was chipped from ice and stone. "Fine, I'll bite. Who are you. What do you want."

"I have what I want, James. You, alone, in a nice empty train car on a lonely stretch of track. I've been following you for weeks now, waiting for just such a golden opportunity. And now that it's here, I really couldn't be more delighted."

Indigestion

A sudden flurry of movement in the darkness, as Halligan plunged his hand into his coat: Banks remained still, waiting with a smile for the fat man's frightened grunt.

"The pistol? Long gone, I'm afraid. I removed it from the holster when I stumbled into you, as we were returning from the lounge car. Rather obvious, you know—such a big nasty bulge under the jacket."

"Whatcha gonna do?" Halligan growled.

"Oh, nothing much," Banks said airily. "Just wait, really. In a few more minutes, my work here will be done. I'll step off the train in Toledo, and that will be that."

"If you're gonna try and kill me, little man, you'd best make your play," Halligan said. The seat squealed under his weight. "I'm ready for ya."

Banks shook his head. "I've already done all I need to, James. To be perfectly honest, I could have walked out of this compartment five minutes ago and you would still be dead within the hour. But I never dreamed you would be so obliging as to take *three* of those antacid tablets. I'm afraid that the effect of the poison will be…rather less subtle than I had hoped."

With a sudden roar Halligan rose to his feet, blundering across the chamber to crush Banks beneath his weight. The thin man moved with incredible speed. He sprang out of the way, ducking out from under the lunge just before Halligan's body crashed into the wall.

Squatting on his heels on the opposite seats, he crouched over the heaving back of his victim, his teeth bare and shining. Halligan slumped on his knees, his upper body draped over the seat in which Banks had been sitting. "A little unsteady, are we?" the thin man asked—his voice still lightly conversational. "Understandable. Halidol is nasty in large doses."

For a long moment, the chamber was silent, except for the tortured rasp of Halligan's heavy breathing. With an irritable sigh, Banks finally stepped down between the wide trunks of Halligan's legs, took him by the shoulder, and rolled him back, letting him slump onto his side on the floor. "Yes, too quickly," he said, disappointed. "That was the last gasp of your voluntary muscle control, James, and I imagine you must be feeling very cold right now. I had rather hoped you would last a few minutes longer, but no matter. I just wanted to tell you, before you die, that you are by far the most repulsive, brutal slob that it has ever been my considerable pleasure to kill. Your lovely wife was willing to put up quite a sum for my services—but honestly, I would have taken this particular commission for free."

He shook his head in mock sadness. "Poor woman. Surrounded by thugs! Hard to imagine that her own father would marry her to a gelatinous mound like you… and all because you were willing to pull a trigger on command." Banks shook his head. "Shameful, really, that they call themselves a 'Family'. Don't you think?"

The thin man stood and straightened the seams and cuffs of his suit. "Imagine what that must be like," he mused. "Being married to 'Jimmy the Whale'. Having to lie next to a thing like you." He nudged the rasping mass on the floor with his shoe. "Insult to injury, James, that you couldn't be faithful to her. All the way to Chicago, to visit your mistress? But I suppose that's what passes for subtlety, to a hit man."

Banks stood at the door a few moments more, until at last the tiny room was silent. He knew when the final moment came, could see the terminal shudder that passed through the 400-pound carcass on the floor. An unpleasant odor quickly rose in the enclosed space—*eau de chilidog*, which not even the sulfurous grit of the factories could overpower.

It was the smell of acid indigestion.

Three Desert Poems

On Lying Down

Keep moving.
Stop to rest,
Sit down in the desert,
And they'll circle above,
Sailing on the updraft
Like black scraps of ash
in a hot chimney wind.
Goaded perversely
By such keen anticipation
of my imminent end,
I have often lifted my burden
Before I was ready
And traveled on

଼ ଼ ଼

Waste

In this place,
coyotes eat from garbage cans
and every rib is picked clean.

Things do not rot secretly
as in the wet woods—
bodies don't stay buried long.

It is an imperative:
nothing is to be wasted...

When all have had their share
even the carcass of a great beast

Leaves only a sand-scoured skull,
grinning…

Or an ant-picked femur
That the wind plays, like a flute.

☙ ☙ ☙

The Mirage

There are three sacred rules
in the wasteland:
do not spill water
do not look in the sun in the eye
and do not let good things pass you by untasted.

I cannot understand what you have done.

You emptied your canteen,
and filled it with whiskey:
but whiskey doesn't kill thirst—
it only numbs the need.

You looked up into the sun at noon
And let the burning truth blind you—
But like all great truths,
the sun didn't blink
and now there is no one to lead you home.

I would offer you a sip from my canteen
I would offer to lead you
I would offer even myself…
but I am only a fellow traveler:

tired
dusty
sweating

Three Desert Poems

scorched
and lamentably real...

I cannot compete
with your madness,
with that shimmering beauty
that you have seen
on the horizon.

ICHTHYS

The room was found at 4:00 p.m., just minutes before the swing shift whistle. The great drill suddenly hit a wall of stone. Monteverdi, the day operator, had long ago lost his hearing to the roar of his earth-boring machine; still he managed to stop the drive mechanism within seconds. Many years underground had taught him to listen to the TBM with his bones, not his ears—he felt the change in vibration instantly, as if his own teeth had bitten into a piece of aluminum foil.

In the single moment it took him to pull the lever back to a full stop, the drill ripped through two feet of stone and mortar and screamed triumphantly in the open air of a long-buried chamber. The damage was done. Monteverdi cried a warning: the wall crumbled, a cold exhalation of stifling, centuries-dead air rushed past his face, and the men of the day shift echoed his shout as a cascade of red earth and loose stones showered from the roof of the tunnel.

The shrill cry of the drill slowly trailed away to a low moan, and silence. It was this, as much as anything, that brought the foreman running. "What's happened, Monteverdi? Are you all right?"

The old man nodded. He pointed to the hole in the tunnel wall ahead, not bothering to speak, and the foreman swore bitterly.

"*Deo canne!* Not again?"

"*Si, Signore.* Stone, then air; it is a hollow place."

The foreman shook his head in disgust. "Back the drill out of the way," he said. "We'll send for Father Macchi."

The archeologist came from the ancient catacombs to the newly excavated subway tunnels on foot. Summoned by phone, it was still almost forty minutes before he arrived at the work site. He had come the whole distance at a trot, carrying a heavy can of lacquer in one hand and a pack over the opposite shoulder. "Where is it?" he gasped. He bent and set down his gallon can, then took off his hard hat to wipe his brow; thinning hair stood up in angry tufts around his balding pate.

"The place is here, *Padrone*," Zadora said. He handed the priest a lantern and pulled up the corner of a plastic tarpaulin, which had been rudely hung over the breach. "Only Trochino and I have been inside. We tried to save it from the air, as you said, but…"

The foreman of the subway's digging crew would not meet his eyes, and Father Macchi knew that it was very bad. Bracing himself, he ducked under the tarp and stepped down into the room.

It was a small, square chamber, walled and floored in stone. In the far corner, the surveyor, Trochino, stood silently. Macchi had met the man before, but never paid him much attention—he was cut from much the same cloth as the other workmen in the tunnels, a short, bandy-legged man with the bull neck and thick shoulders of a digger. Now, however, Father Macchi could see the man's dark eyes were filled with genuine anguish.

"Too late," he whispered hoarsely. "Too late, Signore."

Macchi raised his lantern high, illuminating the whole room with its electrical glow. Three walls were still standing intact, paneled all around with marble friezes. Each metope had been painted with a vivid scene; it was as if eight lively windows had opened from this room. The oldest known style of Roman painting, and seldom seen; the place must have lain undisturbed since a full century before the birth of Christ.

Everywhere he looked, however, the once-bright paint clung to the walls in ashen tatters. The pigments were darkening and peeling away even as he watched. The atmosphere of modern Rome had done its work quickly—in less than an hour, the hot living air of the tunnel had eaten up everything that the cool dead calm of two millennia had managed to preserve. Now the ancient paintings were burning in an invisible fire, crisping and curling, falling away from the wall in tragic flakes.

Macchi did what he could, working with a delicate brush to coat the remaining images with preservative, collecting the larger flakes of the paint with a pair of tiny tweezers. While his lacquer dried, he used his digital camera to take as many pictures as possible of the room and its walls, the stonework of its domed ceiling and the few stairs leading upward to an earth-choked doorway.

The foreman waited while Macchi measured the room and recorded its dimensions in his little notebook. "Well? What do you think it is, *Padrone*?"

The priest shrugged sadly. "A sleeping chamber, perhaps. Very old. They may be able to date the paintings from the samples I've taken. Unfortunately, the images…" He winced and let the words trail off.

"It's directly in our path," the foreman said pointedly. "Trochino here has done a survey of the ground nearby—this was a single room. There are no other stone walls beyond it."

Macchi turned to the surveyor. "Is this true?"

¶CHTHYS

Trochino cleared his throat and nodded. "*Si, Padrone*," he said. "We are very deep here, far into the earth. This one room was at the bottom of a long stairway. There were no rooms beyond, and no house above."

Macchi sighed. "Yes. The stairs which once led to it collapsed, and it was forgotten." He turned to both men with the next question. "Tell me—did you look at these paintings, before they were so badly damaged?"

Zadore avoided both the priest' eyes and his question, but the surveyor spoke up quickly. "*Si, Signore*. I did." Trochino took off his helmet, holding it in his hands—like one speaking of the dead. "I am very sorry they would not wait for you."

The priest pursed his lips. "Was there a boy with a harp, by any chance?"

Trochino nodded. "Yes. The pictures told the story." He pointed to the stone panels on the three standing walls as he spoke, indicating a scene painted on each metope. "A musician, whose wife died of snake bite. She was buried, but he led her back from the Land of the Dead." The surveyor looked at him with open admiration. "But how did you know, *Padrone*?"

Macchi pointed to an image still dimly visible on the wall. It was the figure of a woman, dressed in a flowing white robe, a long veil hanging down over her face. "I thought I recognized the lady," he said simply. "Her name is Eurydice—the boy with the harp was Orpheus, who later became a god of music and poetry." He looked down at his notebook and quickly scribbled a few more words.

Zadore shifted his weight uncomfortably, but said nothing. Trochino met the foreman's eyes and turned back to the priest, trying to speak casually. "Would you say that this an important finding, *Padrone*?" he asked.

The priest made a face. "It might have been. Very little is left to study, obviously. But I have seen a room like this once before, in Rome—many years ago, when I was a student. A sleeping chamber, deep underground, with a secret stair leading down to it. It was tiled, rather than painted, but it also depicted the myth of Orpheus."

The foreman cleared his throat. "What shall we do, *Signore*?" he asked. "My crew is waiting."

Macchi removed his spectacles, cleaning them with his handkerchief as he deliberated. "Remove the panels," he said at last. He put the glasses back onto the bridge of his nose, his face settling into long-familiar lines of stubborn resolve. "Have your men pry them from the walls as carefully as they can. Clear the debris from the room with brooms. Empty all of the earth into boxes, so that it can be sifted. And tell Ferrero at the museum and Professor Standhope at the University what was found; the two of them can come and see if there is anything worth keeping."

"And then…when we have done all this…we can continue?" the foreman said.

"And then you can continue. I have been told that you cannot stop work for everything." The priest shook his head. "I must be getting back to my own digging now."

Zadore bowed his head. "Thank you, *Padrone*."

Macchi shrugged. "It is nothing. Thank you for calling me. I am grateful. I only wish I could have come faster."

"There will be a faster way," the foreman said proudly, "when we are finished with the subway."

Macchi's lips curved in a thin, cheerless smile as he bent to pick up his can. "Of course."

The priest made his way back through the press of workmen and their machines, a stooped lonely figure in his black frock and wire spectacles. He had not gone more than 100 feet from the work site, when he heard the clump of booted feet behind him.

He turned to see Trochino hurrying to catch him, clutching a brown paper bag in one hand, holding his helmet onto his head with the other, his tool belt flapping at his hips with each step.

"Yes, Trochino?" Macchi said, as the stocky surveyor skidded to a halt. "Have I forgotten something?"

"No *Padrone*. Only my work is done for today, and I thought perhaps you should not walk back to the catacombs alone."

Macci frowned. "Are the tunnels not safe?"

Trochino made a dubious face. "In truth—no, *Padrone*. The second and third shift workers have had some trouble lately. We cannot find the place where they are sneaking in—but we know things have been stolen."

Macchi took a deep breath through his nostrils and then sighed aloud. "Yes," he said at last. "We have had similar troubles. I think they are only vagrants from the city above, come down to seek shelter at night—the artifacts in the tombs are never disturbed. They take only tools, or food which has been left behind."

"In any case, *Padrone*, one never knows. Perhaps not all of these vagrants are so harmless." Trochino shrugged. "It is safer for two men to walk together, no?"

Father Macchi nodded and continued walking, inviting the surveyor to come along with a tilt of his head. "Of course. It is thoughtful of you to offer. Still…" He made a quick gesture to encompass the workman's passage, with its electric bulbs strung along the ceiling and wooden planks laid end-to-end in the red mud at their feet. "There are streets above which are not nearly so well lit and hospitable."

The surveyor nodded. "Very true, *Padrone*."

"Rome is not what She used to be," the priest said.

"No, *Padrone*. The city is rotting, like the souls of its people."

Macchi gave the surveyor a sharp glance, surprised, but nodded in agreement. "Perhaps you are right, Trochino. People often ask me if I am afraid, when I am alone among the dead. But I am far less afraid in the tunnels than in the city. Rome is becoming more dangerous every day. Even a poor divinity student is no longer safe."

Trochino walked beside the priest, hustling to keep up with Macchi's long stride. "Student, *Padrone*?"

Macchi nodded grimly. "One of our young assistants disappeared a few months ago, at the beginning of the summer. He was from an American university; he left work one evening and the police say that he never arrived home."

Trochino touched the pendant he wore at his throat. "That is terrible, *Padrone*. And no one knows what happened to the poor young man?"

"No, they have not found him. They thought at first that he might have been kidnapped. But many weeks have passed, and no one has received any demand for ransom. I fear the worst."

"I am very sorry to hear it, *Padrone*. The people of Rome once had true faith—and respect for men of God." The surveyor's voice had dropped a register. "But they are reverting to beasts now. Pagan beasts."

The old priest smiled. "Surely it is not so bad as that, my friend."

Trochino looked up suddenly, embarrassed. "I'm sorry, *Padrone*. I should forgive, I know. But living in such a city can poison a man's soul." The two men walked in silence for several seconds; finally Trochino cleared his throat awkwardly. "Could we talk about the paintings?"

"Of course," the priest said. "Let us change the subject. Did you have a question, Trochino?"

The surveyor tilted up the brim of his hard hat. "*Si, Padrone*. I have been thinking…"

"Thinking is a dangerous habit for a working man," Macchi joked, hoping to set the surveyor at ease.

Trochino bared his teeth awkwardly. "Yes." He hurried on, struggling to force out the words. "Only that it seems a shame, *Padrone*. For such things to be destroyed, as they were today."

"I could not agree with you more," the priest said.

"I was wondering—do you think it would be possible to teach one of the workmen to preserve the paintings, as you did?"

Macchi raised his eyebrows. "One of the workmen?"

"*Si, Padrone*. I wondered if it would be possible to teach one of us—perhaps even a few of us—to save the old things, before the bad air of the tunnels can destroy them. If we were ever to find another such room….perhaps…something could be done to keep the paintings fresh." Trochino rubbed the back of his neck awkwardly, looking at his boots. "Until you arrived," he added.

Macchi pursed his lips and weighed the idea quickly. "It is an interesting notion." He shrugged. "Unfortunately, it takes many years to learn these techniques. They cannot be taught in a day, or even a week—and an inexperienced hand often does more harm than good." He shook his head. "A trained archaeologist should accompany the digging crews as they work on these tunnels—I have asked many times. But no one would listen."

"Not listen—to you? Why would they not, *Padrone*? You are renowned—they say you are the greatest Roman archaeologist in two hundred years."

Macchi waved this away a rueful smile. "I could be the Second Coming of Our Lord, Trochino—it would not matter to the city's planning council. They make many excuses—the inability to guarantee safety, et cetera. In reality, I'm afraid I simply made too many enemies when the new subway was proposed. My colleagues and I opposed the digging for many months." He gave a mild half-shrug of regret. "But you are right, Trochino. It is a great shame. I would very much like to have seen those paintings—especially the images of Eurydice."

"She was the girl who returned from the dead?" The surveyor scratched his beard nervously.

"Yes. The bride of Orpheus." The two men had reached a nexus of tunnels; several passages twisted away in all directions. Father Macchi set down his can again, resting for a moment. "This is my turning, Trochino."

"*Si, Padrone*. I know the catacombs. I grew up in the underground; the men of my family have always been diggers, for many generations."

Macchi paused and took his handkerchief out of his pocket again, wiping the grit from his neck. "Really? That is interesting."

Trochino lifted his chin with a proud smile. "My great-grandfather worked for Rosetti, when they first re-opened the old tombs. He even said that we Trochino were among the first *fossores*, when Nero was emperor. I think perhaps he was exaggerating?"

Macchi gave him a kindly wink. "Perhaps not much, Trochino. Some families in this city can easily trace their lineage back to the old Roman days."

ICHTHYS

Trochino's bright black eyes shone with pleasure. "I would like to come with you the rest of the way, *Padrone*. It has been many years since I have walked in the sacred places. My mother used to bring me here on holy days, when I was a boy, to see the martyrs." The shorter man bent and scooped up the heavy can that Macchi had been carrying by its handle. "Perhaps I can carry this for you, as well." His smile flashed bright in his black beard. "You have already carried it so many miles today…"

The old priest nodded. "As you wish, Trochino. It is still quite a distance to the dig site, but I appreciate the company." He stretched his neck and bent his head to the left, easing the weary muscles of his right shoulder. "And I confess, my old joints appreciate the rest."

The two men turned and took the left-hand path. Like the workman's tunnels, the catacombs were lit by electrical bulbs; here the lights were dimmer, more intermittent. The stone floor beneath their feet was now cool and dry, not churned to mud by the passage of heavy boots and hydraulic machinery.

Long horizontal niches had been cut into the walls of pale, chalky tufa. Empty now, they had once served as resting places for the first Christians buried in Rome. Here and there, a larger gallery opened; in these areas one might find the stately sarcophagus of a wealthy family, or a miniature basilica where a small congregation of secret worshippers once met, centuries before, to celebrate their salvation.

Periodically, the roof was pierced with long vertical shafts which ran all the way to the surface, allowing for a flow of fresh air. For the most part, the way was too narrow to allow the two men to walk side by side, but Trochino stomped along behind the priest, still beaming happily as they walked through the winding tunnel. "Is it much farther, *Padrone*? Perhaps you could tell me about this girl in the paintings, to pass the time."

The priest shrugged, glancing back over his shoulder. "Not much to tell, I'm afraid. The story is an old one. A very talented young man married his sweetheart. She died of snakebite, and was buried. In those days they believed that all of the dead went to the same Hell, regardless of virtue. But Orpheus so loved his wife Eurydice that he could not bear to leave her in that gloomy place. He went before the King of Hell—Hades, of course, not Satan—and begged for her release."

Trochino nodded. "*Si*. I saw this in the pictures. He played the harp for this King of Hell?"

The priest smiled. "Yes. A song of love and grief so powerful that even the God of Death was moved. He allowed Orpheus to lead his bride back up out of the Pit. There was a long stair which led back up to the open air; the only proviso was that Orpheus could not look upon her face until she was back among the living."

"But he looked, did he not?" Trochino asked. "He lifted her veil."

The priest smiled. "So the story goes. He could not wait. As she stood on the threshold, he turned to behold her face—thus breaking the pact he had made with Hades. Eurydice was forced to return to the Land of the Dead. Orpheus had lost her forever."

"A sad story, *Padrone*."

"It is. But an interesting story. And I believe that it may have been more important to the people of Rome than anyone has imagined. You see, I have seen that same image of Eurydice twice now. It struck me very forcefully when I first saw the lady thirty years ago, in another underground chamber; it struck me again today. Eurydice as she appears in these underground rooms reminds me very much of a similar image—one which I see a dozen times a day, here in the catacombs."

The two men had come to another open gallery; the simple frescos painted on the walls had been well-preserved. Macchi paused for a moment, turning to an alcove beside the walkway. "Here she is now. We call these '*orantes*'—the prayerful ones."

The image on the wall was the standing figure of a woman. Her body was gowned in voluminous white, concealing almost all of her form except for the hands and feet. The folds of a veil hung down to conceal her face. "To the Christians, these *orantes* are a symbol for the departed soul," the priest said. "We see the same image again and again—on tombs, in the basilica, on the walls. Look at her, Trochino—is she not the spitting image of our Eurydice?"

Trochino peered at the painting. "I…cannot say, *Padrone*," he said at last. "I am not an expert in such things."

Macchi shrugged. "To me, the resemblance is very striking. More importantly, an *orante* like this one was painted always to represent the happy soul of a Christian. She is the symbol of a person who was buried here in these galleries. The early Christians came here not only to bury their beloved dead, but in a sense to commune with them—an *orante* like this one is often be depicted sitting at a feast table surrounded by the members of her happy family, or celebrating with them in some other way."

Trochino cleared his throat. "I do not understand, *Padrone*."

Macchi turned with a shrug. "No one does, Trochino. It is a strange thing. We have studied these passages and their paintings for nearly two hundred years, but we still do not fully understand the *orantes*. Man, woman or child, the spirit of a departed loved one was always depicted as an adult female, and always wearing a gown and veil like this one. There is a painting in one of these rooms of St. Anthoninus, pierced by a dozen spears—the martyr's bleeding body is on the ground, but the female *orante* is springing up from his corpse with an expression of joy..."

Trochino frowned and squinted at the painting again, as if trying to see some resemblance to St. Anthoninus. "Did the old Romans believe that men became women when they went to heaven?"

Macchi chuckled and continued walking. "I don't think so, Trochino. Not literally, at any rate. No one knows for certain what the *orantes* meant to those who painted them. But many of the words and symbols used in these old places of worship, during the times of persecution in particular, are difficult to interpret. When their faith was forbidden, the Christians learned to celebrate their faith secretly, using symbols as a code. No one could reproach or punish them for painting a simple fish upon the wall—but to the faithful, that fish might remind them of the story of Jonah, the miracle Our Lord performed at the wedding feast at Canaan, or even the name of God. The name of the fish, in Greek, is '*ichthys*'. The early Christians saw in this word an acronym for the name of Our Lord: '*Iesous Christos, Theou Yios Soter*'—Jesus Christ, the Son of God, Savior. Many modern-day Christians still use the Fish as an emblem of faith—even you, Trochino."

Trochino ducked his chin toward the pendant around his neck, and the priest smiled. "Yes," he said. "I noticed your fish right away."

"*Si, Padrone*. 'I believe in God the maker of heaven and earth, and in Jesus Christ his only son, conceived by the Holy Ghost, born of the Virgin Mary. He suffered under Pontius Pilate, was crucified—'"

"'—and buried, and on the third day arose again from the dead,'" Macchi said, smiling. "The Apostle's Creed. Very good, Trochino! You were well-schooled."

Trochino bowed his head. "Thank you, *Padrone*. Would you mind if I stop for just a moment? I believe there is a pebble in my shoe."

The surveyor set down the heavy can of lacquer and quickly unlaced one boot; just as he was bending over to remove it, however, an ominous rumble sounded in the ceiling above. Before he could think twice, Father Macchi had given the younger man a tremendous shove, sending him sprawling forward—just a split second before the roof of the tunnel collapsed.

Sudden, absolute darkness. The priest found himself lying on the rough-hewn stone of the tunnel floor, listening to the ominous boom and thump of stone slabs shifting and collapsing behind him. His legs were trapped, buried in rubble; choking clouds of dust and grit washed over him, and pebbles rained from the ceiling.

Somewhere in the darkness to his left, he heard Trochino try to clear his throat. "*Padrone?*" the man croaked.

"Yes," the priest replied. "I am here."

"Oh, *Dios Mio*," the surveyor said. He sounded so distressed that the priest felt a genuine surge of pity for him. "You are alive, *Signore*."

"Yes," the priest said. "We must remember to thank God later." He took a deep breath and braced himself, trying to move his feet beneath the pile. A few stones shifted around his legs, and brought the dull throb of his left ankle into sudden, shocking focus—he clenched his eyes and teeth tight, the pain bursting like fireworks in the dark.

Trochino shifted somewhere ahead and to the left, sending stones and pebbles clattering as he tried to orient himself toward the sound of the priest's voice. "Where are you, *Padrone*?"

"I'm hurt." Macchi's voice shook, despite his best efforts. "I think my leg may be broken."

From the surveyor's direction came a flurry of scratches and scuffles, followed by another shower of sand and pebbles. Larger rocks rolled away in the dark as Trochino moved closer. "I am coming, *Padrone*," he said. His voice seemed to have risen a few feet from the floor.

"Careful," the priest said. "Do you have a light, Trochino?"

The silent pause that followed seemed almost deafening. Then there came the creak of leather, and the clink and clatter of Trochino's tool belt. Suddenly a circle of light exploded in Macchi's right eye.

The priest raised a hand, wincing. "Please do not blind me, my son."

"Sorry, *Padrone*." Trochino turned the flashlight beam aside, playing it over the heap in which the priest lay half-buried. "We must get you out of there."

"Yes," Macchi said. "But carefully. My ankle."

Trochino wedged the flashlight into a pile of fallen stones and worked with a will, quickly lifting away the broken chunks and slabs of stone which had pinned the priest's legs. "I am terribly sorry, *Padrone*. You were hurt trying to save me from harm."

Macchi winced as his leg shifted. "It was nothing, my son. You would have done the same for me, I am sure."

Trochino stopped for a moment, stricken—then bent and redoubled his efforts to clear the debris. "I would like to think so, *Padrone*. But I am afraid that I am not so good a man as you. Roma has polluted my soul."

"You are a good man, Trochino. Your soul is not polluted; God's love and forgiveness will wash away all of your sins."

Trochino turned and gave the priest a feeble smile. "If you say so, *Padrone*, it must be so. I am sorry that my faith is sometimes weak." The surveyor squatted to scoop away the last of the sand and earth away from the old priest's legs. "I believe we should try to turn you over. Are you ready?"

Macchi nodded, and clenched his teeth to brace himself. Trochino's arms were strong and his touch surprisingly deft and gentle—but still the priest winced as his ankle shifted.

Trochino propped him up in a sitting position, ignoring his grunts and grimaces of pain. When Macchi was upright, the surveyor removed a handkerchief from his pocket and dabbed the cold sweat from the old man's brow. "I am sorry, *Padrone*. Is the pain very bad?"

"Yes," Macchi gasped. "Just a sprain, thank God."

Trochino rose to his feet, looking around. "We are trapped. The catacombs both ahead and behind us have collapsed."

Macchi nodded. "I thought as much. I have been through a few cave-ins before. Usually it happens in new excavations—I could have sworn these passages were well-braced." He shook his head. "In any case, someone will certainly have heard that noise. They will come and dig us out soon enough."

"Yes. I am sure someone will come for us." Trochino turned and found his paper bag in the dirt. "Here; let me give you a sip of wine, *Padrone*. I still have some of the food I brought for today."

Macchi did not protest or resist as the surveyor placed the thermos bottle to his lips; if anything, he was surprised by his own greed, taking it in his own hand to down the remaining contents. The wine was sweet and sharp; he could feel a cool rill dribble down from the corner of his mouth, but did not stop to wipe it away until all the wine was gone.

Trochino had removed a half-eaten loaf of bread from the bag, and now sat squatting on his heels eating it, watching the priest drink with a thoughtful expression. "You were thirsty, *Padrone*."

Macchi took a deep breath. "Yes. Thank you, Trochino." The surveyor held out his torn loaf, offering it, but Macchi waved it away. "No. Is that all you brought for your afternoon meal, Trochino—bread and wine?"

The surveyor nodded, ripping off another chunk of the bread with his strong white teeth. "I had a bit of fruit as well."

The priest raised an eyebrow. "You are a vegetarian?"

Trochino shrugged as he popped the last piece of bread into his mouth. "We are what we eat. I do not wish to be a beast, and so I do not eat the flesh of beasts."

Macchi smiled weakly, fighting down his pain. "You are speaking to a Jesuit, Trochino. Such statements tempt me to debate."

Trochino raised his hands in mock surrender. "I am not so wise as you are, *Padrone*. I could not win an argument. I only know that when I drink the wine of Sicily, I can taste the shadow of the volcano. When I eat a loaf of new bread, the grain of Tuscany carries the memory of rain and sun. The lives of the plants are sweet and full of grace. The lives of beasts are painful, full of suffering and confusion."

"I see." Macchi tilted to his head to one side, studying the surveyor with narrowed eyes. "I have never heard it expressed quite that way before. Very… poetic, Trochino."

The surveyor rubbed his thick hands over his thighs, eyes downcast and embarrassed. "I am no poet, *Padrone*."

Father Macchi pointed to the flashlight, still wedged into a pile of fallen rocks. "May I have it, please?"

Trochino handed him the light and Macchi played it over the surrounding walls. "Interesting," he mused. "I believe the side of this tunnel has collapsed as well as the roof behind us. I would have sworn that section there was a solid wall, but there appears to be more space behind it." He looked at Trochino, licking his lips. "Tell me—do you think there is anything in your tool belt that we could use as a splint?"

Trochino nodded. "I think so."

It took a few minutes to make the dressing; Trochino found a few pieces of broken wood in the wreckage and used them to brace the sprained ankle, wrapping the priest's ankle in electrical tape to secure them. By the time the operation was finished, Macchi was white-faced and shaking.

Trochino looked up at the priest, concerned. "Are you sure we can move you, *Padrone*?"

Macchi swallowed hard. "I think it would be wise. More of this area may collapse; if there are rooms beyond, there may be a safer place to wait for rescue. Please help me to my feet, my son. I think I will need to lean on you for a while."

The surveyor bent and allowed the old man to put an arm over his broad shoulder, raising him easily to his feet. Macchi clung to him with one arm, holding the flashlight with the other to play it over the fallen earth and stone. "Yes," he said decisively. "I have come this way a thousand times. This was not here before." He urged Trochino forward, half stumbling and hopping toward the breach in the far wall. "A new passage has opened."

Trochino remained silent, helping the priest up to the edge of the rubble and standing solid as he leaned into the darkness, playing the beam of the flashlight into the room beyond.

ICHTHYS

"Amazing," Macchi said. "It is an entirely new gallery. Look at the dust upon the floor—how thick it is. Untouched." He turned to the surveyor eagerly. "You must help me, my son. Please, lift me over this obstacle. I must see."

Trochino hesitated, then bent and scooped the old man up into his arms. He carried him lightly over the broken heap of stone like a bridegroom and set him down again, gently, on the other side.

Macchi's flashlight beam played over the room eagerly, darting here and there as the old man's eye took it all in. "What a find! Look at the *orantes*..." His light played over the richly painted walls; the figures of the women in their veils stood all around the semi-circular chamber, facing the viewer with their hands raised in prayer. In the center there was a standing statue, its robes turning in frozen waves of white marble. Its back was turned; Father Macchi hobbled closer, urging Trochino to circle around through the thick carpet of dust.

"Amazing," the priest muttered again. "I don't believe I have ever seen such a sculpture before... it must be an *orante*... but is it Roman—?" His eyes flicked up and down, taking in the details. "Perhaps not. The balance is fine, the pose refined—a Greek artisan, surely..."

Trochino stood silently as the priest hobbled away from his steadying arm, moving closer to the marble lady. "Her gown... the veil... It must be an *orante*. Or is it Eurydice?" His flashlight beam swept upward. "Ah, it has been damaged," he said, disappointed... and then hesitated. "No... the veil has been tied back. Her face... it is—"

Some instinct made the priest turn at that moment, just in time to see the dull white sheen of Trochino's eyes and the flash of his teeth in the dark. Macchi cried out, the flashlight dropping from his hand as he clutched his shoulder—something sharp in the surveyor's mouth had penetrated cloth and skin as easily as a serpent's tooth.

"Trochino," Macchi said. "What—?"

His knees buckled, the muscles and nerves of the legs going suddenly slack. The priest's mouth dropped open as he slowly toppled onto his side, helpless. His unblinking eyes continued to stare toward Trochino, as the surveyor's boots moved toward him across the dusty floor.

"I am sorry to interrupt you, *Padrone*." Trochino's voice was suffused with genuine sadness. "But you are right—someone will come digging for you soon enough. We must go."

Macchi's throat worked silently, trying to speak... but only a low rattle emerged.

Trochino bent and picked up the priest. Now that the room was almost completely black, Macchi could see the way his eyed shimmered in the dark. "I know you must have many questions," the surveyor said gently. "You cannot speak yet because my venom has paralyzed you. It is a gift which my people have; the old Romans believed that we were the descendants of the goddess Proserpina—the first serpent."

He bent as he crossed a threshold, carrying the old man deeper into the tunnels. Macchi's throat made another feeble whine. In the walls here were old sconces, built for torches—someone had hung modern glow-sticks from these, the plastic tubes glowing eerily in the dark.

"I wish I could tell you all about my people, *Padrone*. I know you would find them interesting," Trochino said. "Our men are much like myself—we appear normal to the casual eye, difficult to distinguish from men such as you." He opened his mouth, lifting his thick tongue toward the roof of his palate—and a sharp white thorn seemed to spring forward from the tissue beneath. "We carry a sting, of course. The poison paralyzes quickly—even a younger man would find himself unable to move almost instantly."

Macchi's breath wheezed feebly in his chest.

"But our women are different, Signore," the surveyor said. "The ladies of my race are…more sublime. They live much longer than the men do, and are even more sensitive than we. My mother, my sisters—they could never eat such things as wine and bread."

Macchi's lips quivered, and Trochino smiled down on him gently, his swift stride carrying them further and further into the fluorescent glow of these strange catacombs. "We are what we eat, *Signore*. Please try to understand—we have lived beneath the city of Rome for longer than you can imagine. When we began, we ate the leavings of beasts and wild things—we were little more than wild things ourselves. When the first men came, we hunted them as an animal would. But when the first of our people ate the flesh of yours, our eyes were opened like those of Adam and Eve. We became as wise and cunning as the men of that age."

Trochino's eyes shone. "We lived thus for many centuries. The city of Rome rose high above us, and we rose with it. Through the flesh of its people we tasted the world. We learned a love of finer things. Art. Music. Spectacle. Our tunnels became richer, and decorated with beautiful paintings and mosaics. Sometimes, we found friends in the world above; the gifts of our women were appreciated by a select few."

Macchi's throat worked again, and a single syllable emerged. "Eur…"

¶CHTHYS

"Eurydice. Yes, *Padrone*. When our women partake of the flesh...they take in the spirit of the one who has died. They become the dead, know what they knew, feel what they felt, remember all that they remembered. They can speak with the voices of the ones who were lost. For a grieving man who needs one last word from the woman he loved…it is a great gift." Trochino shrugged. "But of course, she cannot come with him to the world above. And it is always better if he does not lift her veil."

"Trochino," Macchi wheezed. "Why have you—?"

Trochino shook his head sadly. "I am sorry. We never intended that you should suffer; you were not meant to survive the falling rocks. We have almost reached our destination."

The priest's eyes rolled slowly back and forth as the corridors swung past, trying to gain some sense of the paintings—and the dark contents of the niches along the walls.

"Try to understand," Trochino said. There was an note of pleading in his voice that made the old priest shiver. "We did not know that we were sinners, *Padrone*. Eventually the Romans came to suspect our presence, and began cremating the bodies of their dead. My people were reduced practically to animals for many years, able to eat only the offal that was cast from the temples, or the corpses left after a bloody show at the coliseum. We had access only to the lowest sort of men. We were becoming the lowest sort of people ourselves."

Trochino had come at last to an open room; here he finally put the old priest down on a flat tablature of stone. Around the room, a few electric lanterns hung. Macchi's head lolled to the left, and he saw another doorway leading away into the dark. Trochino kindly readjusted his head; the priest was still unable to turn it back on his own.

"One day there was a great event in the hippodrome of the emperor Nero. A vile and evil man, a persecutor of the innocent—but nonetheless, a man to whom my people owe our very souls." Trochino's voice had dropped to a reverent whisper. "In the games that day, a great man was crucified. His head hung low; he died suffering, a mocking parody of another execution which had been performed many years earlier, in Jerusalem."

"S…saint Peter," Macchi said, forcing out the words.

Trochino nodded. Tears had begun to flow down his face. "*Si, Padrone*. It was my great-great-grandmother who brought us the true faith. Through the two Apostles and the martyrs that followed, through the generations of Christians who were buried here, my people learned of the great sacrifice which Our Lord and Savior had made, and of the joy to come in the life hereafter."

Trochino bent low, his voice dropping still further. "It has been hard. Very hard. Faith is dying in the city above us. The people of Rome have once again become low, and cold—interested only in material things. They are poisoning my people—we are losing our faith. And their new digging drives us deeper and deeper into the earth.

"These new Romans are not like the Christians of old. They have forgotten us—and it is better so. They would not understand—would not bring their dead to us willingly, as the first Christians did. They do not understand that we must be saved. Our faith must be kept strong."

Father Macchi struggled to speak. "The student…"

Trochino turned his head to one side sadly. "Yes, *Padrone*. My deepest regrets. His name was James Keller. A talented and intelligent young man, very sensitive. His faith was strong, his love and respect for ancient things even stronger. We have learned much from him—and gained new concerns, as you might imagine."

Trochino frowned. "We too are digging. We must delve deeper, to make a new place for ourselves away from the world above. Like the subway crews, we are finding many ancient and marvelous things—but unlike the city planning council, we have learned to respect them. We do not wish to see them destroyed."

Macchi's eyes suddenly widened. "No…Trochino…please…"

Trochino knuckled the tears from his cheek. "I am truly sorry," he said brokenly. "I had hoped that there was some other way, but you said yourself that your great skill could not be taught to a simple man like myself. There is only one way that my people will gain your wisdom."

Macchi's head lolled to the side once more. Pale shapes were emerging from the gloom, the slim robed figures of women. Their faces were covered by long, sheer white veils—but beneath the fabric, there was a shifting movement which made his skin crawl.

"Trochino…please," the priest whispered. "Not this…not my soul." His eyes rolled wildly. "God help me. God save me!"

Trochino's hand patted his chest, as if to give reassurance. "He will, *Padrone*. You have been a good and honest man. You will sit at His right hand."

Macchi turned his head toward Trochino, but the surveyor was backing away. The women glided silently into the room, and now encircled the stone table. There was a faint, wordless whisper from beneath their veils—a soft, expectant hiss.

One of them was speaking; Macchi recognized the words, although the Latin intonation was strange. "…*From thence He shall come to judge the quick and the dead.*"

❡CHTHYS

The rest of the women joined in simultaneously, completing the final words of the Apostle's Creed in a chorus: *"I believe in the Holy Ghost, the Holy Church; the communion of saints, the forgiveness of sins; the resurrection of the body; and the life everlasting."*

"Amen," Trochino said—but Father Macchi did not. As the oldest of the women lifted her veil, bending to deliver the Kiss of Peace, he simply tried to scream.

Back to Back
(A Valentine's Day Poem)

Sometimes, I get tired
There are too many of them
And the day is long.

It comes at you like an avalanche
You find yourself buried
You've got to hire Price Waterhouse
To maintain the list
of "People Who Need a Slap"...

It's a stinking damn world,
What with everyone taking their garbage to the curb
And no one knowing
Or caring
Where it goes
And who has to pick it up...

"I've got mine."
Those three words
Will doom us all.

Sometimes, I get tired.
There are too many of them!
And the day is long.

I can be brave, because of you.
Tape up my hands again
Cut me if you have to
My fists will fly like angry angels
And no one will take me down.

Arinn Dembo

Back to back
Slowly circling
We'll give them a fight to remember...

It's you and me, baby, against the world.
I'll take the three billion on the left.

The Words

By nightfall tomorrow, I shall enjoy the hospitality of the city police, and I do not think they will allow me the pleasure of writing my own confession. Accordingly, as this may be the last time that I am ever to hold a quill in my hand, or feel the smooth caress of vellum beneath my little finger, I intend to enjoy these small pleasures for as long as I can. Tonight I will write until my tale is done, or until the first light of dawn—whichever comes first. I cannot imagine that there will be an *escritoire* in my cell.

In fact, the confession I intend to give tomorrow will be a false one. The murderer of Edmund DeRoste is beyond the reach of earthly justice, and Monsieur Vidocq will never have the pleasure of clapping the culprit in irons. But someone must confess, and someone must be punished. The damnable man has found me out. I did not succeed in hiding all evidence of the crime. I could wash the residue of poison from a teacup, but not from DeRoste's blood. The inspector knows beyond question that this was not a natural death, and his suspicions have fallen, quite logically, on the one who daily brought him his afternoon tea. DeRoste's servant, poor loyal Jean-Patrice, has been arrested. They hold him pending trial for murder, and I have little doubt that he will hang if I do not take his place.

I cannot allow an innocent man to suffer for my sake. And so, tomorrow, I will go to the prefecture and tell them a shabby lie. They will believe it—it matches my clothes and my station so well—and Jean-Patrice will go free.

Tonight, however, I tell the truth. Someday, someone may understand.

ଓ ଓ ଓ

To the one who finds this little note, perhaps I should apologize. Doubtless you have been at some pains to open the grave of Edmund Auguste DeRoste. I do not know what you hoped to find when you disturbed this earth—playwrights and poets are not known for their great wealth, and DeRoste will be buried with nothing more than a suit of clothes and a few rings. But whatever you were looking for, as you rifled through the pockets of his jacket, I'm quite certain it was not a tin box of letters.

It could be that the centuries have come and gone, and all the wonders in DeRoste's *contes fantastiques* have come to pass: men voyage to the moon and fly through the air like birds, great guns fire bullets the size of houses, and visitors from other worlds are as commonplace on our streets as Americans in their raccoon hats. The reader of this note may not even know who DeRoste was. All his poetry and plays may be forgotten. I would like to think such a thing is impossible, that readers will always love him—but the history of literature is littered with casualties. A man who spoke beautifully to one generation may find no audience in generations to come. Works of great genius may languish unread for decades… even centuries.

His gravestone could last far longer than his reputation, so I hope you already know this much: here lies Edmund DeRoste, born in 17—, died in 18—, *requies in pace*. I can tell you what cold granite cannot. DeRoste was the brightest light of our literary scene, a rascal whose badinage and charm made him welcome in every parlor and public house. His poems made women sigh and men weep; his plays brought forth roars of laughter and of outrage. He fought thirteen duels to defend his essays alone, and won them all. His sword was nearly as dangerous as his pen.

If I tell you he had no peer among the writers of Paris, some might say I exaggerate. *C'est possible.* I loved the man and his words; in truth, I loved the man for his words, and I found it difficult to separate the two. DeRoste himself had the same trouble. Perhaps all writers do.

଼ ଼ ଼

Having introduced the man, I make an awkward curtsey of my own. My name is Claudette Betrand, and I am a person of no consequence. I was born the daughter of a cloth merchant on the Rue Marchande. I was my mother's first and only child; she died forcing my crooked body from her womb. My father, a practical man, remarried quickly to a sturdier woman who bore him two sons with straight legs, and all was right with the world thereafter. If he ever missed my mother, mourned her passing, or saw any resemblance between her and myself, he gave no sign.

When I was a child, my father was occupied with the running of his shop, his wife with the running of the house. I was left to myself. I had no friends, nor a governess; when my brothers were born, my step-mother forbade me to play with them.

The Words

Because I could not walk or run as other children do, I was kept indoors. I could not climb the stairs until I was nearly ten, so I was given a room on the first floor, a small warm place behind the kitchen. The servants were sometimes kind. The cook would let me sit beneath her table with my doll, during the day, and the old gardener was the first to fashion me a little crutch, so that I might walk rather than crawl from place to place.

Fortunately the family tutor, who despaired of pounding letters into the thick heads of my two half-brothers, found in me an apt student of both reading and writing. I was permitted to sit with the boys during their lessons, and because I learned quickly, the tutor made use of me as a goad. When I surpassed them at memorization or maths, he would look down his nose at Bernal and Francois with devastating contempt. If I could perform any task that they could not, he would roll his eyes at them. After the first few months, I had learned to fall behind them in our class—but not before both boys had conceived a lively hatred of me, and learned to play cruel tricks when my back was turned.

They had previously taken no notice of me, but now they would steal my crutch, trip me as I went down the stairs, or perform dreadful surgeries upon my rag doll, Jolie. Strangely, despite these new miseries, I was very happy that year, and in the years that followed. That cross old tutor never knew what a gift he had bestowed upon the crippled daughter of old Bertrand. The books that my brothers abandoned when they went out to play found their way into my room. While they splashed in the muddy gutters, I rode in the company of Charlemagne. While they played with their childhood friends, I was left with Renart and Ysengrin, Villons and Voltaire, Montaigne and Marcus Aurelius, Rabelais and Racine.

As I grew older, my hunger for books grew, and I asked my stepmother for any chore that might earn me a small allowance. When she saw that I was not entirely useless, she let me have a few francs a week for mending. I took my earnings to the market stalls to buy old books, and I was content.

Life continued without much change until my eighteenth year. That was the summer my father took ill. For several months he was confined to bed, and although his senior clerks were experienced enough, he did not trust them to run his business without some supervision. My brothers and I, who had been in and out of his shop all of our lives, were sent to oversee his affairs until he was on his feet again.

My task was to keep the accounts. For three months I sat in a quiet corner with the ledgers, receipts, and bills of lading, while my more presentable brothers attended to our customers on the floor. I was sitting in the very same spot on a cold autumn day when I met the woman who would change my life: Madame Cecile Rosalinde de Maurier.

☙ ☙ ☙

Madame de Maurier was not unknown to me, by reputation; she was one of my father's most precious customers. She was a woman of great beauty, wealth and refinement, a person of influence in Paris. Four times a year she came to our shop with her dressmaker in tow, purchasing cloth for the new season. My father was always careful to order fabrics to suit her unusual needs.

Despite her celebrated beauty, Madame was a widow, and for twenty years she had refused to put away her widow's weeds. Spring, summer, winter or fall, she always wore black. The key to her taste was to find the black silks, black lace, black organdy and woolens which yet carried some appealing pattern—stylish but not garish—which would serve to make her wardrobe fashionable, rather than funereal. A brocade of golden chrysanthemums might please her in winter; a sweep of pale gray doves might take flight across her skirts in spring.

In any case she was widely admired, and her dressmaker was the most expensive in Paris. Where these two shopped, others flocked after them; accordingly, keeping her custom was a matter of great concern to our father. When she arrived unannounced, only two weeks after having purchased several bolts for the winter season, my brothers and I were seized by dread.

"Madame de Maurier!" Bernal cried. He and Francois tumbled over one another like puppies in their haste to take her dripping umbrella. "What an unexpected pleasure. How can we be of service—?"

"A small thing." Her voice was soft as a snowflake. As she walked into the shop, she unpinned her veil from the brim of her hat, revealing her legendary face. Even in her late thirties, she was an incandescent beauty—her heart-shaped visage framed by ringlets of beaten gold, her figure as slim and straight as the heroine of an old romance. As she came nearer and nearer to my perch in the back, my heart sank lower and lower. When she at last stood before me, I placed a ribbon into the book I had been reading and tucked it under the counter, facing her with a feeble smile.

"Good morning, Madame," I said—or tried to say. My throat had closed; I could barely force out the words.

"Good morning, Mademoiselle Bertrand." Her voice was gentle. Surprised, I looked up into her eyes, and found that they were deep lapis blue—and smiling.

"Ca-can I help you, Madame?" Desperate, I looked to either side, trying to summon my brothers for aid.

"I believe you can." She reached into the pocket of her skirt, withdrew a small purse and opened its silver clasp. Inside, there was a folded slip of paper. She placed it on the counter: a receipt from our shop. "Did you write this, Mademoiselle Bertrand?"

Bernal and Francois both glared at me, their eyes burning suspicion. *What have you done, Claudette*? I looked down at the bill, trying with all my might to see what fault there was to find with it. Had I added incorrectly? Had I charged her for more than she bought? I could not see my error, whatever it might be. "Yes, Madame. I am responsible. Is something wrong?"

"Not at all. I could not help but notice that you had a very fine hand, Mademoiselle. Such lovely script is rare." She withdrew a few 20-livre notes from her purse and tapped the receipt with her fingertip. "I'll pay this now, I think."

"Yes Madame." Numb with relief, I took her money and made a few francs of change. "Thank you, Madame."

She slowly drew a black glove back on to the slim fingers of her left hand. "You read books as well, *ma cherie*?"

My cheeks flushed red with embarrassment, I could only nod.

She smiled. "Very good. I was certain you did. I must tell you: a situation has recently opened in my household. I find myself in need of a companion and lady's maid. If you are at all interested in the position, I would happily offer it to you; I have known your father for many years, and consider Monsieur Bertrand an excellent reference."

Thunderstruck, I sat staring. It fell to my brother Francois to answer her, after a few awkward moments of silence.

He cleared his throat. "I'm sorry, Madame. I don't believe our sister is able to do such work." He nodded toward my cane, leaning in the corner. "You must not have noticed—Claudette is a cripple."

A ripple of expression passed over Madame de Maurier's face, and her head tilted slightly to the left. It was a gesture I learned to recognize in years to come, a pained silence with which she greeted some word or deed so gauche that she could not bring herself to acknowledge it. She paused for a moment, and then continued exactly as if Francois had not spoken. "I believe I can offer you an attractive wage, Mademoiselle. I hope you will discuss it with your father. If he can spare you during this difficult time, I would be most appreciative."

She gave me her card; I took it with a shaking hand. "Please let me know as soon as possible." Taking her umbrella from Bernal, she let herself out of the shop. I could barely understand what had just happened, but I clutched the little rectangle of fine paper in a vise grip.

☙ ☙ ☙

A situation. A companion. A lady's maid. The family was in shock; from the moment I was born, it was assumed that I could be nothing in life but a burden to others. The notion that I was welcome in the home of a fine lady of good family and estate was inconceivable.

My stepmother was the first to recover her wits and seize the day; she knew better than to miss the chance to have me out of her house. The following morning, she dressed me in my most presentable clothes and took me to see Madame de Maurier. I don't believe I said more than two words during the entire interview—my father's wife answered all of Madame's questions. When the subject of my duties arose, Madame turned to me and handed me a book: I recognized the author immediately, a favorite of the old tutor.

"Claudette, if you would please turn to "Perseverance", and read the last lines aloud?"

I bent to the familiar task. I could barely speak at all, if the words were my own, but losing myself in Balzac was easy. Without a moment's hesitation, my voice rang out clearly:

"… *Nevertheless, this wealth, far from emptying his purse, filled it full to overflowing, because so rapidly increased his fame and his fortune that he was able to buy a patent of nobility and lands, and he founded the house of Anseau, which has since been held in great honour in fair Touraine.*

This teaches us to have always recourse to God and the saints in all the undertakings of life, to be steadfast in all things, and, above all, that a great love triumphs over everything, which is an old sentence; but the author has rewritten it because it is a most pleasant one."

Madame de Maurier smiled. "Very good, Claudette. You will do very well indeed."

"She has the job, then?" my stepmother said. "You will take her?"

"Indeed I shall. Thank you, Madame Bertrand. You have done me a great kindness; I hope you and your husband will accept a small token of my appreciation." With this, Madame handed across a bank draft. I did not see the sum, but my stepmother's eyes flew wide and beads of sweat sprang up on her nose.

"Thank you, Madame. You are very generous. You know my husband has been ill…"

"Yes, Madame Bertrand."

"Things have been very bad."

Madame de Maurier nodded. "I pray for your husband's swift recovery."

"I have two sons, if ever you have need of—"

Madame cleared her throat. "Thank you, Madame Bertrand." She picked up the little bell upon her table and rang it; her valet appeared at the door. "Please bring the coach around to see Madame Bertrand home safely." My father's wife was shown to the door, still bobbing and nodding her respects. "Claudette will join her in a moment."

I was left alone with Madame, my stepmother having accepted the job on my behalf without so much as a glance in my direction. Cecile de Maurier smiled at me. "Come, Claudette. I have made a place for you, if you will have it."

She led me up the stairs to the second floor. It was part of her natural grace that she found a way to ascend those steps so languidly that it did not seem that I lagged behind her. When we reached her private apartments, she opened a white door.

If I had entertained any doubts about entering her service, the sight of my new bedroom erased them. It was easily four times the size of my closet at home, with a soft bed and a tub for my own private baths. A vase of bright flowers had been arranged on the bedside table, and a few paintings of pleasant country scenes upon the walls. In the corner, there was a writing desk and pair of tall bookcases. At the sight of them I forgot myself and hobbled forward.

I let my fingertips trail over the fine gilt and leather spines. Moliere. Shakespeare. Cicero. I had read many of these before, but I had never touched a book so elegantly bound. I leaned close, intoxicated by the mingled perfume of good paper and leather.

"I had intended to remove these shelves later." I turned to her in sudden fear; Madame de Maurier's eyes danced, and the smile she offered was so beautiful that tears sprang up in my eyes. "But I will leave them, if you like."

I nearly threw myself at her feet; I was in the presence of an angel, a saint. "Please, Madame. I…I would like to read them. When can I begin?"

☙ ☙ ☙

There was nothing else to it. My few possessions were thrown into a single box, and moved into the splendid room. For the first year I did not unpack them, hardly daring to expose my tattered books in Madame's fine house, or show the face of poor Jolie. I was fitted for three new dresses, simple and sober clothes which echoed Madame's own. I became a member of Madame's household, paid twice monthly. I was allowed half a day's leisure on Tuesday afternoons.

My duties were simple. I awoke before Madame, sorted her letters and newspapers, and brought them to her with her morning meal. While she drank her coffee, I read her correspondence aloud, and then sat at her desk with pen and paper as she patiently dictated each response. Afterward, I helped her dress and arrange her hair; I would remain at her side for the rest of the day, departing only when dismissed. If she was alone or with intimate friends, I might even take meals with her. And when the mood struck her—as it did quite often—I would read.

I was, quite simply, Madame de Maurier's eyes. Her vision had begun to fail in recent years, until even her best reading glasses were of no use. The attempt to read a finely printed line would make her eyes water and her temples throb; a note from a friend, the menu at a restaurant, the program of a play, and a bill from the grocer's were all equally painful. But half of her life was in correspondence, and in her social circle it was impossible to enjoy the company of others unless she was prepared to discuss the latest novel, poem, or pamphlet. As her companion, my duties were light—but indispensable.

At the end of the day, I would brush her hair until it shone like a cataract of yellow silk, and plait it into a long smooth rope. She closed her eyes, rested her head on the pillow, and I took whatever lay upon her bedside table to read aloud until she was ready to snuff the lamp and sleep.

It was there, seated on the edge of Madame de Maurier's bed, that I first encountered the love of my life. I had just read a sheet of hand-written verses, two sonnets so scandalously funny that I laughed aloud—and at the bottom of the page, I saw his name: C. Edmund DeRoste.

☙ ☙ ☙

"Cousin Edmund", as she called him, had been a fixture in the life of Madame de Maurier since she was a small child. He was her second cousin; the two of them

The Words

had played together on the family estate in the Dordogne. They had always moved in the same social circles, and when he joined the musketeers, the two remained close. He had been a good friend to her husband, in years past. After Monsieur de Maurier was killed in the war, DeRoste remained one of the very few intimates with whom Madame could discuss her husband—and the only one before whom she would openly weep.

The fact that he was one of the most celebrated littérateurs in Paris was an afterthought, to her; Madame was aware of his fame, but she never seemed to understand it. To Cecile de Maurier, DeRoste was only "funny old Cousin Edmund", and she could not regard him in any other light. He always passed along his latest efforts to her, long before they were published; she received his poems and plays with a gracious smile, but she was careless about reading them. Celebrated as he was, his cousin found his work... uninspiring.

Naturally, I had heard of DeRoste before. It was impossible to haunt the bookstalls in any marketplace without hearing of his latest escapade. He was the sort of man that people love to talk about, and his latest writing was always avidly sought—so much so that I had never been able to read more than a few discarded leaves which fell when another customer had taken the last copy.

When I first came to work for Madame de Maurier, he was away from the city for a number of months, on holiday in Italy. Thus I had nearly half a year to find every page he had written and read them all—once or twice aloud, at her direction, but more often secretly, in my room. It became a delicious treat to search the voluminous sheaves written by her other friends, when Madame was away, seeking these little treasures... always written in that vigorous, back-slanting hand which I came to recognize at a glance.

By the time I was nineteen, I knew a page written by DeRoste anywhere, not only by sight but by sound. Every line was spoken by the same wonderful Voice. To me, these were the outpourings of a great soul: wry, sad, irreverent and wicked, world-weary and wise, sweetly romantic, and often given to rage—this last always on behalf of those weaker than himself, who were wronged by the strong. His pen had a Voice, and when that Voice spoke, I burned. I could give no name to the passion that had come over me. I took his unpublished poems and hid them under my mattress, as if they were written for me.

His letters came more frequently as he planned his return to Paris. Day after day I sat at Madame's desk, writing her calm and courteous replies. I was unbearably excited that he was coming back—that he would soon be as common a visitor in Madame's parlor as any other friend. But how would I recognize him? None of his published books carried an engraving of his face, and much as I searched, I could find no portrait of her cousin among Madame de Maurier's things.

The reason for this became clear soon enough. He sent word that he would call on her, on the fifth of September. On the day of his arrival, Madame took me aside.

"My cousin Edmund is coming this afternoon. Since you have never met him, I must warn you that he is a man of great sensitivity. Please be very careful not to stare at him. He is very tender about his looks, and quick to take offense."

I nodded and lowered my eyes. DeRoste—was he ugly? Could such wonderful words be written by an ugly man? I allowed it could be so. I understood ugliness well enough, having borne its curse all of my life. I had certainly heard the tales of DeRoste's quick temper. The notion that I could offend or insult him in some way terrified me. But part of me marveled at Madame's tone—did she really think her Cousin hideous? She seemed to have a very tender affection for him; she always began her letters to him "Dearest Friend"... could it be that she was as kindly solicitous of his deformity as she was of mine?

I sat in my accustomed chair by the window when his carriage arrived. From this vantage point, DeRoste was nothing but the crown of a broad-brimmed hat, its band sporting three long spotted plumes. When I heard his thunderous knock, heard the thud of his boots on the wooden floor, the rumble of his approach in the hall, I thought he must be a giant.

The door opened; the valet spoke his name. He exploded into the room like a flock of pigeons, sweeping off his hat with a bow. Before Madame de Maurier could more than half rise from her chair, he had clapped his arms around her and kissed both her pale cheeks.

"Cecile, *ma chere cousine!* I am home." And with that he collapsed on her divan, as if he had run the whole way from Italy on foot. Before Madame could speak again, he launched into the story of his travails on the road from Tuscany. Anxious, I waited to be introduced, but it was impossible; he stayed for two hours, and in that time poor Madame could not get in a word.

I contented myself by studying the man from the corner of my eye, stealing longer glances when I thought I could go unnoticed. Vainly I searched for ugliness, beginning with his face. It seemed a good face to me. A firm Gallic nose, perhaps a bit larger than usual, which served him as a ship is served by a strong prow. An old dueling scar across the bridge was more romantic than disfiguring. A generous mouth, filled with strong white teeth. A lavish moustache, lustrous black, and a neatly pointed tuft of beard upon his stubborn chin. He wore his hair long, in glossy, coal-black curls—another man might have paid handsomely to wear them as a wig. Large, soulful brown eyes, surrounded by lines of laughter and pain. Thick lashes and brows—these as mobile and mercurial as a summer sky, portending joy or thunder with his many swiftly passing moods.

Finding no ugliness above the neck, I continued my search below. DeRoste was not a tall man; he wore a high-heeled boot that came to his knee, but when Madame stood to greet him, she had to bend to kiss his cheek. His shoulders were broad and powerful beneath his cotton chemise, the sleeves rolled up over a sun-blackened forearm. His hands had seen both hard work and violence. He had the thighs of a horseman, and a prosperous middle—but these did not seem to me unattractive.

Despite myself, I found myself caught up in the story of his roadside adventures, which he told with such passion that the voyage seemed as marvelous as a trip to Arabia. I found myself riding upon the waves of his voice, having lost all sense of time or self—smiling and often almost chuckling as he talked, as if he were speaking to me directly. But at last, concluding his narrative, he leaned forward; Madame de Maurier smiled as he took her tiny hand.

"And so I return to Paris, not much the worse for wear. Sweet cousin…" He kissed her fingers. "You are looking well."

She squeezed his hand, smiling tenderly. "I am well, *cher* Edmund. I am glad to see you again." She met his eyes. "You are, indeed, not much the worse for wear."

He smiled broadly. "Fortune did Her worst the day that I was born." He stood to go. "But tell me, before I leave—who is this little person sitting in the corner? She has been staring at me ever since I arrived in the rudest, most reprehensible manner!"

With that he turned to me, full face, and gave me a broad comedian's wink. Caught! My mouth dropped open, aghast. I jumped to my feet. The blood soared to my face in a ferocious hot blush.

"This is my new companion, Mademoiselle Bertrand. I took her into my service several months ago—she is quite precious to me." There was a note of chiding in Madame's voice. "And I'm quite sure that she was not staring at you, Edmund. Do not be diabolical. Poor Claudette has never stared at anyone in her life."

DeRoste, grinning, made a florid bow in my direction. "*Enchanté*, Mademoiselle. I am delighted to make your acquaintance. She who is precious to Cecile, is precious to me."

I could not speak; instead I made a sharp, sudden bend of knees as a curtsey, and took an abrupt interest in my shoes.

"And now I am off." He clapped his flamboyant *chapeau* back onto his head. "Good day, fair cousin. I may call on you again next week, if you will have me."

Madame laughed and stood to see him out. "But of course I will. You know you are always welcome."

His last gesture was an odd one, repeated countless times in the ensuing years. Madame waited for him at the door, and DeRoste turned toward the mantle. There above the fireplace was a painting of Monsieur de Maurier, before he went away to war; DeRoste squared his shoulders and heels and gave his old friend's portrait a quick, jaunty military salute. Then, without another word, he left the room.

☙ ☙ ☙

I continued in Madame's service for another four years without incident. Her cousin Edmund was a regular visitor and a constant companion to her. She could call on him any time; DeRoste attended her at the opera, escorted her to concerts and plays, joined her for luncheon and rides in the park. As I grew older, and saw more of the world—or rather, that small part of it which passed through Madame's drawing room—I understood more and more how she depended on her cousin to shield her from other men.

It was both Madame's joy and her grave misfortune that she had given her heart to only one man in her life. This was the gentleman whose portrait hung above her mantle. She did not intend to re-marry, and could not bear even to be courted—whether for her beauty or for her fortune made no difference. Even to hear the suit of another man was an insult to the memory of her beloved Lucien, and she would not allow the subject to be broached. Twice I saw her cut off all contact with a man who dared to make an improper suggestion—all letters returned and all visits refused from the hapless fellow thereafter.

When she thought she was alone, Madame often mourned for Monsieur de Maurier. More than once I saw her reach behind that portrait and take out a packet of letters, still bound by a faded ribbon. Many of them remained unopened, even years later—but in one of the old linen envelopes, there was still a single lock of his chestnut hair. On her darker days, she would open that envelope and breathe in the smell of her beloved, hold the silken loop of hair against her cheek, and weep.

From time to time I studied the portrait of Monsieur de Maurier myself. It was impossible to do otherwise, when he was the object of so much love. He was a handsome young man, in many ways the masculine counterpart to Madame's own luminous beauty: tall, lean, with piercing gray eyes and features so lovely they might have been a girl's. His face did not seem unkind, and he looked well in his uniform. But whatever quality he possessed that could inspire Madame's lifetime of devotion, I could not see.

There is little else to say about those years, save that I was happy. My hunger for words had never been so gluttonously surfeited: I drowned in books, papers, letters and writs. Soon, emboldened by my daily service to Madame, I began to write little things of my own, in my private hours. My salary was more than sufficient to afford my own quills and a bound diary; in the pages of those blank books I began to explore my inner country.

I burned those diaries this evening; I could not allow them to be found. Someone might have seen in them a contradiction with tomorrow's confession. In any case, all those little thoughts had no great value; in all the years I sat writing, I arrived at only three great truths.

One, that I was desperately and hopelessly in love with the great writer, Edmund DeRoste.

Two, that Edmund Deroste was just as hopelessly in love with my mistress, Cecile de Maurier.

Three, that Cecile de Maurier had given her heart away years ago, to a dead man, and would not ever return her cousin's love, no matter how great their mutual affection. Her love for him was of another nature entirely.

I suppose that in my simple way, I had assumed that these great truths were equally evident to all three of us. I thought we had agreed, by silent mutual consent, to continue as we were; we knew there was no need to trouble one another with painful subjects, or to speak of loves which can never be returned.

As it happened, I was mistaken. The three great truths were known only to me, and neither Madame nor DeRoste understood and accepted them as I had. Apparently, there are some matters in which a crippled serving girl has the advantage over a great beauty or a great talent, and the acceptance of pain—both for myself and others—was one of these.

☙ ☙ ☙

The change in DeRoste came slowly. It was obvious to me that he was restless, gnawed from within by a pang that grew stronger with the passage of time. Unless he found some relief, it would eventually become unbearable.

Last November, he announced that he was writing a new play. "It will be my greatest work to date. The one for which I am remembered."

"Really?" Madame lowered her knitting. "And what will be the subject?"

"Love." He fixed her with his eyes. "It will be a comedy."

"Excellent! I shall look forward to reading it."

DeRoste began the same evening. The writing was the work of three months; he did not call upon Madame during that time, although she sent letters to inquire after his health. When I delivered the last of these to his door, following Madame's own instructions, Jean-Patrice would not let me in.

"He is working," the old man said simply. "He is not to be disturbed."

The play arrived on a stormy February evening, carried by Jean-Patrice in an oiled leather sachet. I brought it to Madame still dripping from the rain. When she bade me open it, I found the play itself prefaced by a terse note: "Cecile—please read. I will call on you tomorrow to see what you think of it." Unusually, he had signed it with his first name: "Anxiously yours, Charles."

"Well!" Madame took the heavy parcel from my hands, hefting the weight of the five acts within. "He sounds very urgent, *n'est ce pas*? We shall have to begin reading this at bedtime, Claudette—it won't do to be rude."

"No, Madame." I was outwardly calm—but I could barely contain myself. What on earth had DeRoste written in this play, so urgently, so passionately, for three long months without rest? What was so important that he could not wait a single day longer for Madame to read it?

The answer was slow in coming. Madame's guests lingered over their coffee; Madame herself dawdled on her way to bed. Even as I braided her hair I could see how tired she was, her neck bowed like the stem of a wilting flower. She lay in bed ready to listen—but by the second page of the first act, she was sound asleep.

Quietly I snuffed the lamp, took up my cane, and retired to my own room. I still held DeRoste's play under my arm. Cecile de Maurier might be too tired to receive his words, but I was born for nothing else. There was not the slightest possibility that I could sleep before I had finished reading that play. The sun might sooner fall from the sky like a lemon.

And so I sat, first with laughter, then with tears, and finally in cold, sickening dread, as I turned page after page. It was, indeed, DeRoste's masterpiece—a magnificent play about a magnificent man and a magnificent, tragic, and beautiful love. It sparkled with fine *repartée*, with humane understanding, with affection and tolerance for all the pretty foibles of humankind—moreover, with an abiding faith in the deeper truth which lies beneath the face we all must show to the world.

At last I read the final words, so hastily written that the ink had not been properly blotted. He had finished it that very evening, I was certain, only hours ago. Even now he was pacing, sleepless, waiting for the hour when he could come to Madame, and demand her answer.

The Words

Silently, I took up my candle and went to the parlor. For the first time I dared to touch the portrait of Monsieur de Maurier, drawing aside the picture frame to find the packet of letters. Looking constantly over my shoulder, I took them to my room, and opened the ribbon with a trembling hand.

No. No, even from the very first letter, there could be no doubt. Even had the Voice not spoken so clearly, the occasional backslant of the hand would have given it away. Shaking, weeping, I opened one after the other—even daring to profane those which Madame had left sealed and unread, all those years ago.

When at last I was finished, my heart was cold; foreboding hung over me like an axe. Only a few hours remained until dawn. I worked as fast as I could; I had an ample supply of Madame's best paper at my disposal, and I knew her epistolary style very well. I referred often to my own diaries, scanning page after page for all the things I had longed to say, but had never dared. I knew it must all be voiced now… every precious word. There could be no holding back.

ж ж ж

He arrived the following afternoon. Madame could not conceal her delight; of the three of us, only she was not ragged for want of sleep. Seeing the hollow, feverish gleam in his eyes, I trembled. Nonetheless, he greeted her with a smile. "Cecile."

"*Bon jour*, Edmund. It is so good to see you again—congratulations. You finished your play!"

He took her hand and sat upon the divan, drawing her down into the chair beside him. "Yes, *cherie*." He looked into her eyes, searching. "And did you read it?"

Madame looked away. "Of course." She was ashamed, naturally, but so eager to spare his feelings that she couldn't bear to tell him she had fallen asleep. "It was good—very good! You should be quite proud."

A smile broke out, bright as the sun piercing the clouds. "Do you think so? I had hoped… hoped that it would speak to you."

"Oh yes." She nodded. "Very much so."

"Ah Cecile." For a moment, overcome, he bent and pressed his forehead to the back of her hand, as if in supplication. "I should have written it years ago. When I think of all the time I wasted…!" His voice was heavy with emotion.

Tenderly, Madame tousled his hair. "Your life has not been wasted, cousin. You have written so many fine things… this is only one of the many."

He sat up abruptly, looking into her face. "Surely you cannot mean it." Incredulous, he laughed. "Cecile, this play *is* my life...your life...even poor Lucien's life..."

Madame's back stiffened. "Lucien? I'm sorry...I don't believe I understand. Was one of the characters supposed to be Lucien?"

He gaped at her. "Of course. Lucien, you, me—you didn't see it?"

Madame withdrew her hand from his with chilly finality. "No."

Something seemed to pierce him at that moment, as if an unseen shaft had feathered his breast; unwittingly he put a hand to his chest. "Cecile." Her name was a plea. "Surely you remember, years ago, when Lucien was courting. The letters he wrote to you...the many love letters...?"

"Yes?" She frowned; she did not understand, and was not certain she wanted to.

"Those letters won your heart, did they not? Lucien...the loving words he wrote...?"

"Ah!" Madame suddenly smiled again, and patted her cousin's hand affectionately. "No, Edmund. Of course not!"

He froze, one hand still clutching his chest. "No?" Numbly, he added, "Not?"

"Not at all." She wrinkled her nose prettily. "Lucien was never good at writing letters. He was never himself when he picked up a pen; he'd go stiff as a board, and try to be flowery—it was dreadful, really. His letters always made me laugh. He tried so hard to be poetic!"

"But..." DeRoste turned helplessly toward the painting on the wall. "You've kept his letters, haven't you? For all these years...why?"

A mist of tears rose in her eyes. "I've kept everything, Edmund. Anything he touched is still with me. His clothes, his comb, his scissors. I would sooner throw myself into the Seine than lose any of his things. I may not love the letters, but I loved the foolish man who wrote them—a man who believed that a simple soldier was unworthy to love me. Who tried so hard, for my sake, to be something better."

I watched, eyes burning, as the blood slowly drained from his face. At last he stood. "Cecile...forgive me." He offered her a painful smile—God, could she not see? "I have been very foolish."

She shook her head, smiling in return. "Not at all, cousin. We so seldom speak of Lucien." She lowered her eyes, and her voice dropped as well. "The pain is so fresh, even after all these years."

Moved by an impulse of kindness, he caressed her cheek with the back of one finger, brushing away a tear that shone like a dewdrop on a morning peach. "I…I would like to read those letters of Lucien's." He turned toward the portrait. "If you would not mind."

She made a dismissive gesture with one hand. "Take them all, if you like. I know you loved him too. But don't think too unkindly, please, of his mawkish pretensions, when you read them—he was a very young man, trying so hard to please."

DeRoste paused in mid-step on his way to the mantel; I could almost see where the second shaft had driven through him. "No." He practically staggered to the mantle. "Of course…I will not judge him too harshly."

As he reached to take the bundle, she suddenly lifted her chin and held up a hand to forestall him. "But leave me one. The one that still holds a lock of his hair? I cannot part with that one."

"Just the one," he murmured. He gave her the bundle, and she quickly withdrew her prize—sparing not a glance to the other letters, much to my relief.

"Yes, you can take the rest—they are only words. The words do not matter."

Throughout this interview, I had remained in my corner, as dumb and helpless as a rag doll. But when Madame de Maurier loosed the final, fatal shaft, I rose to my feet, a storm of protest rising in my throat—too late. Already DeRoste had turned to the man above the mantel, offering not his usual salute but a final, low bow of defeat. He left without another word.

His carriage clattered away in the street, and Madame de Maurier turned to me, still holding that single envelope in her hand. "You are dismissed, Claudette." Tears glittered in her eyes. "I must be alone. You may have the rest of the day to yourself."

I turned and hobbled from the room. I had just seen Madame do more harm with a wrinkle of her nose than a dozen men with swords could have done in a pitched battle, but I had no thought to reproach her. At that moment, only DeRoste mattered to me, and I knew that I must reach him.

I went to my room, searching for the money I had saved. It was not much; I had been liberal in my book-buying the week before, and now I silently cursed the fine volumes that no cab driver would take in lieu of coin.

In the street I offered money to the first carriage that would stop for a serving girl with a cane; he took it and left me less than half the distance to DeRoste's house. It was nearly an hour before I could limp the rest of the way, running as best I could upon a twisted leg. By the time I rapped upon the kitchen door, night was falling, and it had begun to rain. My leg was on fire with the unaccustomed exercise.

"Letters for Monsieur DeRoste," I gasped, the rain still dripping from my matted hair. Jean-Patrice held out his hand, but I shook my head. "Very *private* letters. Madame… Madame insisted that I give them to him personally."

Jean-Patrice nodded, a knowing smile in his eyes. "Take the back stairs," he said, indicating the narrow servant's way from the kitchen. "His study is the second door to your left."

I struggled up to his rooms, and returned only a few minutes later. If I was a bit pale, Jean-Patrice did not seem to notice. "He… he says he will be writing," I told him. "He does not… wish to be disturbed."

And with those words, I went out again into the dark. By then, I did not feel the rain.

ଓ ଓ ଓ

Now the sad bells are tolling, and half the city is wearing a black band on one sleeve. The great man is dead, and he lies in Monmarte, his casket heaped with wilting lilies. Everyone has been to see him, as if to reassure themselves that it could be so—that a man so vibrantly alive could now lie cold in a gilded box.

I have been to see him myself. Once I stood beside Madame du Maurier, biting the inside of my cheek as the slow tears flowed beneath her veil. I dared not look down into his coffin. She reached out one hand, still encased in its silken glove, to touch him; the *curé* took pity on her for a moment before he said gently, "*Non, Madame*. You musn't," and put a stop to it.

She tottered away like a woman twice her years, my hand at her elbow. I guided her to the nave—she lit a candle for his soul, and I led her home. Though my eyes were dry and my teeth clenched tight, there was still a little room in my heart for pity. Cecile de Maurier could not know what she had done. She understood only that her oldest and dearest friend in the world was gone.

The second visit was made alone. The other servants thought me callous to demand my usual hours of leisure when our mistress was so stricken. But I could not bear to be in the presence of Madame de Maurier a moment longer. I put on my hat and coat and went out into the streets once again in the rain—heartily wishing that the cold water coursing down those gutters would rise and wash me into the river.

I had no plan, but nevertheless my feet were carrying me back to Monmartre. In the end, they found me standing over him, transfixed.

The Words

The mortician had made DeRoste a stranger. I memorized that face in life, learned its language, mapped its every mood and season; there was not a single line, not a twitch or a tremor that I could not read. But now his brow, once creased by frequent thought and pain, was smooth and white as a cake of soap. His eyes and lips were sealed mindlessly shut. And by some arcane mortuary art, they had eased the final anguish from his face—giving him a false, painted peace that real death had not.

As I looked at him lying so placidly upon his back, his hands folded neatly over his breast, I remembered how I had seen him last: convulsed upon the floor of his study, his eyes still wide and bright with accusation. His lips drawn back in a rictus of agony, his teeth flecked with tea leaves; the cup and the killing bottle on his desk beside a single sheet of paper; and shattered in his death grip, the pen with which he had written his final, enigmatic line.

Once I have placed these letters in his casket tomorrow morning, I shall tell the inspectors that I poisoned the great Edmund DeRoste. I will show them the bottle I spirited away from his room. Confess to having washed his cup, and dashed the smell of almonds from his mouth with a dribble of anisette. I will admit that I had loved him in secret and add that he spurned my affections—I'm sure he would have, had I been fool enough to offer them.

Of course they will believe me. The club-footed servant girl, dark and ill-favored, harboring her curdled passion until it drove her to madness? *Oui, c'est doux*. It will please the inspector very much, I think. It is a good story. The world believes that an ugly woman is capable of anything.

Madame de Maurier will grieve. She may curse and despise me. I am content, so long as she never learns what was written on that final page, by the light of old letters burning in a grate. I do not want her to know that his last desperate act was to spit those dreadful words she spoke back out into the world's cold, unfeeling face:

"Because the words do not matter."

෴ ෴ ෴

That is what he wrote.
But it is not so.
Already there is talk about his final play—that heroic tale of an ugly man with a beautiful heart. If the world remembers no other labor of his pen, I am sure that this one will linger long in memory. It will teach a thousand women to choose a man for his soul, not his face. It will give a thousand men the hope that they can

be loved for what they are, and not merely what they appear to be. And thanks to Claudette Bertrand, no one will ever know that the author of this wondrous work recanted the truth he had found in the brittle glass of his most cherished illusion. No one will know that he despaired, and declared that words did not matter—after he had so gallantly proven, for once and for all, that words are the only thing that do.

Let them take my head. I have read Edmund's final page, and it broke my heart to cast it into the fire. I can do nothing now but save Jean-Patrice, who was loyal and true, and leave the man I loved with these letters, written in a desperate hour. My only comfort is the joy they might have given him, had they arrived in time…

…signed, as they are, with the name "Cecile".

The Crown

The old man went into the woods that day
To hunt up some meat for his ailing wife,
And when he was away, she sprang up quick
Half-dancing on her crippled, wooden toes
And hobbled to the stove.

                          There were four good eggs
Hidden in a chink, and flour, sugar
Butter, orange water and all the rest
Ready to hand, so she began to bake
And sing a little song.

                          In a humble pan
She made a nest of flour, and four eggs
With knotted hands she mixed the batter well
Using a spoon he had carved for her
From a black cherry bough.

                          'Twas a moment's work
To rake the coals and set the pan to bake
In the stove that kept their little hut warm.
Shutting the latch, she turned the hour glass
To measure out a cake.

                          She had no warning,
For the dogs had gone hunting with her man
In the yard, a mounted horseman waited,
Leaning on the stallion's neck, chin in hand
As she croaked out her joy.

Arinn Dembo

                    Forgive my trespass,
He said. I followed thy voice to this glen;
It is the first human sound to greet me
Since I came among the silver trees
Of this strange forest.

                    She fell silent then,
And her old heart hammered at her dry ribs
Like a ring-mailed fist at the bedroom door.
She scarce remembered how to kill a man
It had been so long.

                  But please do sing on,
He said. I hardly know why I came here,
A fool on a fool's errand, far from home,
But your song has been the first to soothe me
Since I was a babe.

                  You must remind me
Of a nurse I loved when I was little,
But who was gone before I knew her name.
I was passed from hand to hand as a child,
Like a hot coal.

                  Perhaps you can help me?
I came to this wood seeking my father
But I have lost my way, and my horsemen
And until I heard your singing, I thought
My wits had gone as well.

                  Who was your father?
She asked. *There is no one here but us two.*
So I see, he said. I had hoped for more,
But I am a fool on a fool's errand;
They said so at home.

The Crown

        He took out a coin,
Stamped with the likeness of a former king.
Here is my father, he said. A second:
Here is my uncle, who died at my hand.
A third, new minted:

        And now, here am I.
I carry these three crowns with me always.
They change nothing, excuse no sins of mine,
But being one of three kings struck in gold,
I know my worth.

        He held out the three crowns
And she took them in her crooked brown hand,
With such loving care, such tender caress,
That the young king turned away, disgusted,
Taking it for greed.

        Here was her husband,
In his youth, his glory: Gods, how handsome!
Even gold could hardly do him justice.
With her thumb she stroked his shoulder, his neck,
His elegant beard.

        And his brother, too
Plucking the wings from angels in heaven
Now that his earthly pleasures were all done.
Bitterly she scarred his cheek with her nail,
Hissing with old hate.

        Take them back, she said,
Hardly able to look at the horseman.
He took her wrist and held it fast, saying:
Tell me what you know, mother, and quickly.
It can do no harm.

>   If I find him here,
> I will restore him to his rightful place,
> And follow him as I was meant to do—
> Ascend to take the throne as his first-born
> With hands as white as snow.
>
>   She looked at him,
> This king, and read his face with a queen's eye.
> He was hard; there was no mistaking it;
> He had learned to work his will by slaughter
> And sign his name in blood.
>
>   A regicide,
> She thought, he has killed one king already.
> What is another old man's life to him?
> What does he think his father's rightful place—
> A palace, or a grave?
>
>   *Your Majesty,*
> She said, *Forgive me that I knew you not,*
> *But I am seldom visited by kings.*
> *You are the second monarch I have seen*
> *In this forest.*
>
>   *Your father has been here*
> *These many years,* she said, *among the trees:*
> *He is the master of this winter wood*
> *Of bears and wolves, of rabbits, silent snow*
> *And cold twilight.*
>
>   *Ride on but half a league*
> *And you will find him by the riverside,*
> *For that is where he fell. We buried him,*
> *My man and I, beneath a heap of stones;*
> *'Twas a full day's work.*

The Crown

                        How came he to fall?
It was his brother's doing. Twenty men
Rode through the wood, and burnt our cottage
And killed our George when we gave them no aid
In their treason.

                      The king's rage was so great
At seeing us abused, that he came out
From where we'd hid him and our Lady Queen
And made a great slaughter of the blackguards
In that very glen.

                        We gave him our help
As best we could, with simple farmer's tools
But in the fight he was sorely wounded
And he fell down bleeding among those he killed.
He died soon after.

                        What of my mother?
Asked the boy, the king and killer of kings.
Did she live, or did she die the same day?
I think she had half-died before she came,
Your Majesty.

                      When her son was taken,
The little prince she bore with so much pain,
The hope of the kingdom, even the world—
I think she lost her lantern then, my Lord,
And all was darkness.

                        She cried out for him
At night, and went into the woods weeping,
And with her breasts still full of mother's milk,
She cast herself into the black river
To be carried off.

                            The king turned away
And went to lean upon the saddle horn
With his head upon his forearm, silent.
Dear God, he said, had I but known!
He could have suffered more.

                            It was too quick.
How I wish I could kill my uncle twice!
Undeserved mercy is still divine,
She said, half-regretting what she had done.
It cleanses the soul.

                            Perhaps you are right,
He said at last. When God counts out my sins,
It will already take a day and night.
A slow death for my uncle, though deserved,
Would only damn me twice.

                            I will go now
And take my father's bones where they belong
To a good tight tomb made of noble stone.
I thank you for your service to the crown
In keeping his grave.

                            Some reward
Is overdue for such great loyalty.
Now that you are so old, and cannot work
Perhaps you would like to come back with me
And live in some comfort.

                            We thank you, sir.
But we were only servants to the throne
And did little enough for the kingdom.
It is reward enough to be alive
And together.

The Crown

       This humble hut we have,
These woods and waters, beasts and silent trees
They are a little kingdom in themselves,
But without the war, and want, and treason
That bedevil real kings.

       You are content.
It seems strange, seeing this hunter's hovel,
But I heard your song, and do not doubt it.
He mounted then, and squinted at the sun:
Not long 'til noon.

       Your Majesty, she said,
If you will grant me but a simpler boon—
The golden crown you carry, of yourself:
Could you spare another? 'Twould please my man.
He always wished you king.

       Welcome to it,
He said, and tossed it on the window sill.
She watched him go, and raised her voice to sing
The same cradle tune which brought him to her
Across the long years.

       When her man came home
He found her at the table, with her cake,
And he put a pair of spring rabbits down.
As he sat, they both spoke up together,
"Today I saw our son—

       He has the crown."

With Much Love for my husband, on Valentine's Day 1996

Sacred Heart

I remember the first time I held her in my arms.

Eyes closed, arms wide, air streaming through her fingers—instinct demands that you try to catch yourself, even when you fall thirty stories. She had not given them the satisfaction of crying out. Her lips were still pressed stubbornly shut. That harpy shriek in my ears was the wind, whirling her hair into my face like a thousand silken whips.

I took a split second to match speed with her descent, held out my hands, turned her body and gathered her gently to my chest. I cradled her, slowing her fall, drawing her warm weight closer to me. I could smell her skin, the sweetness of lotion, the spice of fresh soap. Feel her thundering heart against mine. Glistening tracks ran from the corners of her tightly shut eyes, along her temples and up into her hair, the wind-blown tears of mortal terror.

At last we hung in space, still ten meters from the ground. At last she realized that she was no longer falling. She opened her eyes, and saw me looking down at her.

For the first time since I was a boy, there was not a single doubt in my mind. All my questions were answered. Why was I born a freak? Why was I given these powers? What were they for?

At that moment, I knew: I was born to save her. I needed no other reason for being.

☙ ☙ ☙

Who was I? A lost boy who grew up to be a lost man. My parents died on Grey Day, crushed aboard a city bus when a cloverleaf on the 610 collapsed. My *abuela* raised me in one of the few houses still standing in the Third Ward. Every weekday I passed the whispering wreckage of the Grey cruiser that had smashed most of the Trey, skipping along like a massive discus taking out whole neighborhoods with each bounce.

My *abuela* had powers, but she used them quietly. Her flowers and vegetables were the best on the block. If a neighbour invited her for coffee, someone in the household was sick—and would soon feel better. She used her abilities to pay for the uniforms I wore to Santa Maria del Corazón Elementary school and she taught me not to draw attention to myself. Under her raven eye I tip-toed through childhood and stumbled through youth, learning very little about who and what I was.

Who was the falling woman? Her name was Glenda Morgan. She was a reporter for the Star Tribune. She had been working on a story about organized crime. On that day, the story came to her…and dangled her by the ankle from a rooftop, demanding she name the source of her information on their rackets. Glenda Morgan would not give them a name. When the threats and the pain didn't persuade her, they let her drop.

By the time I was through with them, they were broken and ready to say anything to make me stop. I brought them to her, hanging limp from my fists, naïve as a puppy who thinks his blood-spattered prey will please his mistress.

I saw her shudder, seeing what I had done. She had no questions to ask them. She said I should take them to the police station—better yet, the hospital. The way she cringed away, when I came near, struck closer to my heart than a bullet ever will.

I took them to Mercy General. Asked them a few questions along the way. Unlike Glenda Morgan, they found pain and threats very persuasive, and were more than prepared to tell me anything I wanted to know, so long as I didn't let them fall.

Later that night I went to the docks. My power was raging through me like a hurricane. Men flew like matchsticks in the wake of my fury. Over and over I held back the last inch of beating them to death.

At three o'clock the next morning I was at her door, now wearing my uniform, the brim of my cap pulled low to hide my eyes. Excuse me, Ms. Morgan. Sorry to bother you this time of night. There's been an incident down in the warehouse district. The chief thought it might be connected with those stories you've been writing. They asked me to bring you in.

She didn't recognize me, of course. No one ever does. A cop is just a cop, a faceless public servant in blue. Like the garbage man or the mailman, we slide past in a bureaucratic blur. No one looks twice.

Midnight on the worst day of her life. Her violet eyes haunted and hollow, her hands still shaking with aftershocks of terror. Glenda hadn't changed out of her clothes, hadn't eaten, hadn't slept—still rattled by her brush with oblivion. It must have taken an incredible act of will to pick up that tape recorder and come with me, but she did. We arrived just in time to hear Vladimir Komarov confess.

Sacred Heart

The story made the front page. The editor gave her a corner office. Glenda Morgan went back to work, writing about crime and corruption, addiction and poverty, injustice and greed. She was using her powers…but not quietly.

☙ ☙ ☙

Let me explain: prior to that night, I was nothing.

I couldn't fly. What I could do was really more like…floating, I suppose. I would rise into the night sky like a soap bubble, slow and unsteady and shaking in the wind. I would drift unevenly in the direction I wanted to go.

I wasn't a costumed hero, either. I was hanging above the downtown core dressed in a tank top and a pair of sweat pants. My only nod to anonymity was a wrestler's mask, something I'd thrown in the closet three Halloweens ago. I wasn't there to help anyone, or even to look in anyone's windows or steal. I just wanted to look down on the shining city.

That all changed in a thunderclap when I saw Glenda falling. I went from floating to flying in a split second. It happened so fast that the air shattered and the sonic boom shook the windows for a ten-block radius. I didn't know what I was doing, what I could do, until I was reaching out to catch her.

I left her on the roof of a six-story brownstone. The wind screamed past me, a wordless shriek in my ears. I was hurtling toward the roof and the faces of the men who'd dropped her, moving faster than I could think, faster than I could understand—moving at the speed not of thought or of plan but of feeling. Power raged through me, ripping me apart like lightning, like madness, like falling in love. I didn't know myself. Didn't know what I was going to do. I only knew I had to catch them. Had to hurt them.

When it was all over, I drove back to the silent house I had shared with my grandmother. I stood in the dark kitchen where she had roasted *chiles* and rolled *tamales* and I stripped off my uniform in the grey dawn light. I sat huddled in *abuela*'s old claw-footed bathtub all day, hugging my knees and shaking uncontrollably.

I couldn't understand what was happening to me, couldn't cope, couldn't accept. Instead I clung to Glenda. Night after night I hovered outside her window, just above her line of sight. I watched her sit at the keys until the wee hours of the morning. I memorized the messy tangle of her brindle curls, the curve of her neck, the sound of her voice. I found myself drawn into the passing show of her life, certain that I had some part to play. It worried me to think of her riding the subway alone at three a.m.. On my nights off, I couldn't sleep until I knew she was home safe. On the shifts I worked, I found myself slipping way more and more often to put on my suit and check on Glenda.

It wasn't a real hero's costume. A police force as big as the Jacktown PD arrests a lot of guys in long underwear over the years. Some are hero wannabe's who lash out and get caught. Some are two-bit villains who wash out on their first bank job. The costumes they wear go into the evidence locker, and after the trial or the psych assessment they go into storage. No one ever looks at them again. We've got boxes in the precinct basement that go back to the 1930's. If a pair of gloves goes missing from one box, a pair of boots from another—who's to know?

If Glenda had gone to the window and looked up, she would have seen me silhouetted against the moon. She could have watched me come slowly into focus over the course of weeks, like a photographic print in a bath of chemicals. But hardly anyone ever looks up, in this city.

03 03 03

I was there the night her crusade caught up to her again. She was walking toward the train station. They were young, hungry, the kind of dogs that skulk in alleys and nose around garbage cans, looking for scraps. I saw them from the sky above, slinking out of the shadows as she passed; dark shapes, silent and quick, their white masks pale as bone in the moonlight.

Right away I knew it was all wrong. Too many, too quick, too quiet, too well coordinated. This was no shambling pack of pups out looking for a random thrill—a purse to snatch, a set of hubcaps to boost, a door to kick in on a Saturday night.

No. They knew who and what they wanted. They had been paid well to lie in wait.

The leader moved in, reaching for the bag at her shoulder. Glenda wouldn't let it go. She always carried her notes with her, in a portable hard drive in her shoulder bag. Too many times she had returned to find her home or office in a shambles, her equipment smashed or wiped clean. She stumbled and fell, still clinging to the bag. Standing over her, I saw him raise his fist.

I was already moving when he barked his command. Two of his goons closed in on her, knives gleaming. I hit the first one so hard that he still doesn't remember his name. The other is in the state penitentiary, and I hear he's turned to Jesus.

Three more waded in from the sides, raising their weapons. "Get the mask." The growl of the leader was too low, rolling over itself like the rumble of a big cat. Inhuman. "The woman is mine."

Glenda cried out as one of them swung a 12-pound sledge at my head. Her cry turned to a strangled gasp when the hammer glanced off my shoulder with the low musical ring of metal on metal. I gave him the back of my hand. He hit the wall with a shower of brick dust and slumped, already unconscious.

The blade of an axe rebounded from my chest. I took a low vicious swing under the handle; the boy's body wrapped around my fist like pizza dough and he sank to his knees, wheezing. I knew he was done, would black out in seconds. It's what you do when your solar plexus is paralysed.

"All right, flyboy." The rumbling low voice spoke again; I turned in time to see him drop Glenda's arm and beckon me with both hands. "Let's dance."

The alley behind him boiled with shadows. This one had power. He had made some pact with the living darkness in the world, and now it was a part of him. I could see the way black smoke crept out of his leathers, enveloping his body in a killing cloud. Even as I stepped in to engage, I could feel it crawling over me, gnawing—trying to unravel my skin and my soul with a thousand whispering voices of pain, fear, doubt.

I knew I would have to finish him fast. I had no experience fighting another mask. I swung with all my strength; he ducked the punch and stepped inside my guard. His fists became a blur, pummelling me with a dozen blows in an instant. I reeled back a step, my guts on fire. When I coughed, I tasted blood.

"Aw…" He sneered in mock sympathy. "Did that hurt, underoos? What'sa matter—can't take it?"

I could sense the ugly smile behind the voodoo mask. He held out his hand and made a sudden yanking gesture in the empty air. My whole body went ice cold, and my heart slammed against my breast-bone like it wanted to burst right out of me.

He was winning. The bastard was winning.

Through the drifting clouds of killing smoke, I saw Glenda's face. The light of hope in her eyes was dying, rapidly crumbling to despair. I was her only champion, her only chance; if I fell, she would be alone. With him.

Images flashed through my mind, each one worst than the last. His fist raised against her. Those hungry shadows swallowing her. Glenda's fear, Glenda's pain—Glenda's blood.

A red mist rose before my eyes. Rage was coursing through me, and for the first time in my life, I let it come willingly. At that moment, I didn't just want to beat him; I didn't just want to stop him.

I wanted to rip him apart.

The floodgates of power burst wide open, and the red rage coursed through me. He cocked his fist to swing again; I landed a blow to his midsection that would have dented the grill of a Mack truck. He doubled over, fighting for breath, and I brought my fist down onto his shoulder so hard that his clavicle snapped like a twig.

"Whats'a matter, Smoky?" I gritted through my teeth. "Can't take it?"

He raised his head, trying to gather himself for another flurry. I whipped my fist across his face backhanded, striking with everything I had. He flew down the alley and skidded into the trash. I saw him writhe in the garbage, trying to get back up; just as he regained his feet I let him have another savage punch in the gut.

He crumpled to the pavement, unconscious. His shadows fled, scurrying away from their master to hide again in the cracks of the world. I stood for a moment, hands on my knees. Turning to Glenda, I finally asked, "Are you all right?"

"They took it." Her eyes were shining with angry tears. "They took m-my bag…"

Following her gaze I saw him, just rounding the bend at the end of the alley. The last skinny jackal in the pack, running full-tilt to make his getaway. I left the ground at speed and piled into him from behind, a flying tackle that sent him sprawling. One last vicious jab in the face was all it took. I opened his jacket and recovered Glenda's battered handbag, still none the worse for its adventure.

The sound of running footsteps. Glenda was coming. I handed her back the purse, and her face lit up with such joy that I couldn't help but smile back. I gave her a grin that made her face crumple with disbelief and horror—behind my mask, my teeth were painted with blood.

An awkward silence grew between us. Finally she stammered out a few words. "Tha-thank you. Thank you so much. You have no idea…wh-what this means to me…"

"I have some idea, Ms. Morgan. You've been working on some big stories lately." My voice was a wheezing rasp. I cleared my throat, trying to sound less like a guy who just got his ass kicked. "Even us 'pyjama-clad vigilantes' read the paper."

She blushed a ferocious shade of red. "My God. I did say that, didn't I. I swear, I will *never* use that phrase again—in print or in private."

I smiled, slowly rising into the night sky. "Write whatever you want, Ma'am. I like your column. Read it every day. Just try not to be out alone so late at night—ok?"

"What's your name?" she shouted after me, as I disappeared over the rooftops. "Which hero are you?"

ଔ ଔ ଔ

What's your name?

I had no answer to that question.

I'd never chosen a "superhero" name for myself. No one had ever asked me for one. I wasn't registered with the authorities. I was wearing bits and pieces out of the evidence locker at work, a scarecrow made from a dozen third-string losers who had gotten themselves arrested. A pyjama-clad vigilante? Up until that moment I'd always thought of myself as "Juan"—with or without the mask.

As I lay down that night, I tried to imagine something I could call myself. But what do you call a mysterious Latino in a mask and tights? Zorro? All the good names were already taken—if not by other heroes, by wrestlers.

I went to sleep promising myself that I would think of something the next day, but somehow that next day never seemed to come. Weeks and months passed, and I still had no call sign, no identity.

It wasn't until the end that I realized that a superhero doesn't really choose his own name. Eventually a name chooses you.

ଔ ଔ ଔ

Name or no name, Glenda Morgan's guardian angel was a busy man. The woman was relentless. Every day her stories were getting bigger and hitting harder—and so were her enemies.

I was there when she followed her leads out to Gunpowder Cove. I had to face down two regiments of Green Shirts to get her out alive. I followed her to the zeppelin strongholds of the Sky Marshals and carried her through the rain of their burning dreams when she set the great airships alight over the Chihuahuan desert.

I floated high above her as she crept through the cold mists of Flood City, following her flashlight beam through the demon-haunted streets. When the Burning Men took her captive, I waded through so many robe jockeys I could have retired and opened my own textile warehouse. When she followed the blood-soaked bread crumbs left behind by violent eco-terrorists, I had to battle for both our lives against the Earth itself.

I never wavered, never hesitated. Never even questioned what I was doing, or why. Was I fighting with Glenda? For Glenda? It didn't seem to matter.

I followed Glenda Morgan, whatever she did—and whatever trouble she got herself into, I got her out. It didn't even occur to me that she had never directly asked for my help. That she never looked to the sky for my aid. I thought she needed me, and the fact that she needed me was enough. She didn't have to ask. Didn't have to call. I couldn't let anything touch her.

Until he came along.

ങ ങ ങ

I saw them together often, in the first few months. I just didn't see where it was heading at first. He was just another guy at the office, waving as she walked out the door. Holding the elevator for her in the morning. If the two of them stood chatting on the corner at lunch, smiled as they parted ways, who would think it meant anything?

Maybe he watched her a little too long as she walked away, but I couldn't blame him. Glenda was a beautiful woman. If I had to arrest every man who turned his head when she walked by, the city would have been a ghost town.

No, I didn't see it coming, I'll admit. I was too busy scanning the rooftops for the sniper who'd try to put a bullet in her. Rooting in the shadows for the hired thugs waiting to spring the latest trap. I was so distracted searching the crowd for the creep who would whip open a trench coat and pull out an Uzi that I never saw the creep who could sweep her off her feet with a few cups of coffee and a smile.

One night the two of them left the office late. I was waiting on the roof, in my customary watch. I moved into position as the two of them ambled down the sidewalk. Even from a distance I could see the way she tossed her hair as they talked, the way she turned toward him as he spoke. A seed of cold began to flower in my gut, a sense of dread—something I'd never felt before.

When he leaned in to kiss her, I could almost hear the crystalline sound and feel something burst in my chest. I clutched at my sternum, raking the fabric over my heart—suddenly it hurt so bad that I wanted to rip it out. And the air wouldn't hold me up. I was falling, tumbling boneless down to the streets below. I found myself thinking

this is what it feels like to be shot

and then I hit the ground with shattering force. I let myself lie there—my flesh trying to knit itself back together, my mind falling apart. The image had frozen in my head. I couldn't think past it.

Glenda. Kissing. Him.

ଓ ଓ ଓ

Don't get me wrong—I knew I was in love with her. For two years, it had been the simplest, most absolute truth in my life. But it was enough for me to be her champion. I hadn't asked for any greater reward. I rarely even let myself imagine touching her, kissing her. Guardian angels don't ask for kisses. Only mortal men need those.

When I did imagine Glenda putting her lips to mine, I always thought it would be a reward. Something I would receive when I had proved myself worthy. I would hold Glenda in my arms, sailing high in the ocean of wind, and finally she would embrace me. She would put her tiny cold hand to the back of my neck and draw me toward her. She would close her eyes and kiss me through the hole in my shining mask.

She would say I was her hero.

Seeing another man claim that prize was more than I could stand. It broke me in two. I can't even remember how long it took me to crawl back to my apartment. I vaguely recall hauling myself hand over hand with a broken spine up the back alley fire escape to my window. I was too broken to fly.

ଓ ଓ ଓ

I wish I could say that I did the right thing. In hindsight there are a hundred things I could have done, should have done, which would have been better.

I could have looked in the mirror and realized that my motives for being a "hero" were terribly flawed. I could have recognized that Glenda Morgan really did need a protector, but she needed someone who protected her for the right reasons. I could have found a REAL hero—a woman, a happily married man—and asked that hero to take over for me and watch out for her, keep the heat off her back.

I could have looked at the guy she was dating more carefully, tried to find out more about him. Where did he work before he was hired by the Star Tribune? Where did he go to school? Who was his last girlfriend? Where did he go when he wasn't with Glenda?

I could have gone to her. I could have told her how I felt. Regardless of how clownish and tormented and pathetic I thought I would be in her eyes, I could have had the stones to confess. I could have said "Glenda, I love you and I want to be with you" just once, to her face.

I didn't do any of those things. Instead I laid on my living room rug for twenty-four hours, letting my bones knit inch by inch. The day before, I would have shrugged off a fall of less than three hundred feet. If I was hurt, it would have taken minutes to heal the damage. But all my powers were reduced to a whisper; it was as if the door that was kicked open inside me the day I caught her for the first time had been slammed shut. Only a little light was left, bleeding through the keyhole.

I'd also like to be able to say that I never followed her again—but I did. Eventually I recovered from the shock and I crippled out into the night air again. I went to the Tribune, driven by force of habit... and had the pleasure of following Glenda and her new love to an restaurant on 47th street, and then back to her apartment building in Calendar City.

When the light came on in her bedroom, I turned away. Suddenly, I was flooded with rage—burning, unbearable rage. I needed someone to hurt. Badly.

When you want a good fight, you can't beat the Corporation. Any time of the day or night, you can guarantee that they're up to no good. And I've never felt any guilt about hammering a Corp lackey into the pavement. So much of the evil of this world is based on broken, twisted love, or ideals that somehow turn upside-down...but the Corps are the kind of villain who do what they do for pure gain, and nothing more.

People like that, I can beat all day long. I realise it's useless as law enforcement, but it costs the Board a few dollars every time they have to bail one of their goons out of jail or foot the bills at a city hospital. Sometimes you have to take what satisfaction you can get in life.

I don't know how many of them I pummelled that night, honestly. It was well after midnight. I hadn't stopped swinging for hours. I wasn't even listening to their threats and curses, the grunts and squeals and howls of pain. I didn't hesitate for a moment until I found myself holding one by the collar, about to put out his lights, and he said three words that somehow seemed to cut through my crimson haze like a white knife.

My fist froze, still cocked to smash him into merciful oblivion. "Say that again."

His lips drew back over broken teeth, a defiant sneer of satisfaction. "It's too late. We got her. Tonight was the night."

Everything between my chin and my *huevos* went cold as ice. "Got who?"

He was enjoying himself, the bastard. "That Morgan bi—"

My fist trembled, and he stopped himself in time. He looked up into my eyes, and his grim amusement expanded into demonic glee.

"You don't even know." He croaked laughter. "You aren't even on the clock…"

I gave him a shake that nearly snapped his neck. "Tell me everything you know. Now."

"Whatcha gonna do, flyboy?" he leered. "Beat me up and send me to the pen?" He rolled his eyes. "Do your worst. I'm not telling you a thing."

I shot up into the air. "Whatever you say, *cabron*."

His amusement faded as we passed over the towers of the prison and left it behind us, heading out over the Gulf. "Hey…where we going?"

"A little cellar I know over in Flood City." I spoke through gritted teeth, my face drawn back into an inhuman snarl. "I know some boys in robes who are *dying* to meet you."

"You can't do that! I'm…under arrest!"

"Ha! I don't have to arrest you, *cabron*. I don't even have to let you *live*."

"You're bluffing." The fear was in him now; I could hear it in his voice, smell it on his sweat. "You can't do a thing like that. You'd lose your license—they'd whip those fancy tights right off you—"

I turned to him with a vicious smile. "License, *pendejo*? *What license is that?*"

That's when he started to babble. It went on for a while. I shook him a little to speed things up. When he was done talking, I flew as fast I've ever flown in my life—propelled by the greatest fear I'd ever known.

☙ ☙ ☙

I remember the last time I held her in my arms.

I didn't bother with the door; I went straight through the glass. I still remember the way it seemed to hang in the room around me, a million glittering diamonds, falling in slow motion toward the terribly small shape curled under the sheets. That awful moment of hesitation, waiting to see if she would stir. I gathered her up and hurtled back into the night, the wind ripping the tears from my eyes, flying as if I could outrun Death…but He had already come and gone.

I have the same dream now all the time. I'm trying to fly, but somehow the air around me has thickened. I'm moving in slow motion, like a film running at half speed. And in my arms I'm holding the woman I love.

The hospital couldn't help her. She'd been gone for hours. I already knew it, of course; that's why it took me so long to give her up. I knew when I let her go, I'd be letting go for the last time. Part of me would tear away with her when she went. For several seconds I just…couldn't.

She was already cold, terribly cold. The medium who tried to reconstruct Glenda's death nearly went into the mental hospital. She saw the way he killed her, ripping the soul from her body. He wanted to keep her as a trophy. He kept all of them as trophies, their souls like fireflies in little glass vials. He wanted their love—had no use for their bodies.

They call him the Lady Killer.

A special sort of assassin. He specializes in female victims.

The Corporation hired him to do a job. Glenda Morgan was working on a new story—following leads that would take her straight to the spider in the middle of the web. The Board couldn't afford any more negative publicity. Glenda had been after them for a several months already, writing about the petty double-dealing and ominous rumours leaking out of their financial fortress.

So they decided to head Glenda off at the pass, and eliminate a public nuisance. The Lady Killer received the first half of his payment—the money—and he went to work. His reputation still stands. They say he can get to any woman, anywhere, no matter who she may be.

଼ ଼ ଼

For a while after she died, I wasn't much good to anyone.

The trail was cold, and better heroes than I had always been hunting the Lady Killer. I met a few of them at Glenda's funeral—the Dream Merchant, the Stare, Lady Kelvin. I attended in my policeman's uniform; they came in costume. They were there to pay their respects, and sniff around for leads. It would have been ghoulish if they hadn't all lost someone to the bastard themselves.

About a week later, a letter slipped under my door. I heard the rasp of the paper on the wood floor, and got up from the couch for the first time in days to take the three steps to that doorway.

My heart flipped over as I recognized the writing on the envelope. I ripped my door off the hinges, found myself face to face with a frightened kid from the Star Tribune mailroom. He nearly wet himself. It took a few minutes to calm him down enough to tell me where he had come from, and why he had a letter from Glenda.

When at last I understood, I let him go and sat back down. I don't know how long I sat there before I was able to open it. When I did, this is what I read:

"Dear Juan,

If you're reading this, I'm dead. Given the way we usually run into each other, I'm assuming I never got the chance to say goodbye—heroes don't hang around hospitals much, and I imagine I'm going to be in hospice care pretty soon. The medication isn't working too well any more, and I'm in a lot of pain. I don't think I have much time.

I've known your secret identity for a year now. I'm sorry I invaded your privacy—was sorry immediately when I realized who you are, and the real reason you had never registered with the authorities. Conflict of interest. I never would have guessed.

I knew you were a good man. I knew you'd have your reasons. And I've checked—you've never been involved in the prosecution of any villain you caught when you were wearing the costume. You're breaking the rules, I guess, but you're doing it honestly. You keep your two worlds separate. I respect that.

I'm not really sure why I'm writing this now. I suppose I just want to say thanks for all the times you hauled my butt out of the fire. I'd be dead a dozen times over if it wasn't for you. I know you must have helped a hundred other people as much as you've helped me. I know all of us must feel the same way. I've interviewed so many people over the last three years who owe their lives to a man or a woman in a mask, who would give anything to say what I'm saying to you now...to be able to tell the heroes that saved them 'you made a difference'.

So...Thank you.
Thank you for being there when no one else was.
Thank you for doing what no one else could do.
Thank you for taking the beating that would have killed me.
Thank you for being strong when I was weak.
Thank you for putting yourself in the way, when I would have been instantly killed.

Thank you for being everything that a hero should be.

I wish I could have known you better. I wish we could have been friends. But I understand that you needed to protect yourself, and the ones you love. I imagine you must have a family—wife, children. I hope they take pride in what you do, in both uniforms. If they ever wonder whether it's worth the risk, or the hours you're away from home, maybe you could show them this letter. I know I'm speaking for thousands of people when I say: we need you.

Anyway, that's all I have to say. Goodbye. Thanks.

Thanks a million.

Sincerely,
Glenda Morgan"

ଓ ଓ ଓ

Is there any more to tell?

Well, yeah. A little.

Glenda knew the end was coming. She just didn't know how. In the last few months, I've learned a lot about her. Medical records aren't hard to get to when you can rip down a wall—or show up in a blue uniform. Orphanages keep lots of paperwork. Psychiatrists do too. So do oncologists, when the words "malignant" and "metastasis" come up.

Glenda's father was a newspaper man. He died when she was ten. Like his daughter, he was the kind of reporter who would follow any lead, no matter how dangerous. Unlike Glenda, he didn't have a guardian angel.

His loss would have been shock enough for any kid that age, but four months later, the Greys invaded. Glenda lost her mother during their ground attack. Hiding in the splintered remains of the family home, she was the little girl who crouched in silence while her mother broke cover and tried to run—like a ground-nesting bird who can only draw predators away from the babies huddled in the grass by pretending to flee.

Cecily Morgan was ripped apart by Grey rifle fire in front of her daughter's eyes. When they found Glenda in the rubble two days later, she was near catatonic and half-dead of thirst. She hadn't moved since that moment, hadn't cried out for help. For days, she could not seem to do anything but obey her mother's last command: *"Be quiet. Don't move."*

Sacred Heart

When she was sixteen, a field trip to the Star Tribune gave her life purpose. One of the old staffers called out as her tour group walked along the corridor. By then she was a lovely young woman, the spitting image of her mother—except for the piercing blue eyes and the fierce love of justice she had inherited from the old man.

Glenda interned at the paper that summer. She spent hours down in the morgue of the Star-Trib, reading every column and story her father had ever written. By the time the next fall rolled around, she was ready to join the school paper and start throwing her own punches. She had decided to follow in her father's footsteps.

By the time I met her, her condition had already been diagnosed. Glenda, like a lot of kids exposed to Grey technology, had developed an aggressive cancer later in life. Generally it's one or the other: cancer or powers. She drew the short straw. Once she knew, she started working double time. She wanted to make a difference while she was still around. She wanted to help people.

She wanted to save us, having no hope of saving herself.

She was the real hero.

☙ ☙ ☙

When it was all over, I went back to *abuela*'s. She died the year I joined the Force—as if she had been waiting to be sure that I would have a job and a place of my own before she could leave. I stood in her kitchen, under the gaze of her porcelain statue of the Virgin as the sun rose over her garden. The light poured through the glass over the shoulders of *La Guadalupe*. Her white plaster face and the burning jewel of Her heart glowed like holy fire. I can't swear even now that I've ever truly believed in Father, Son and *Madre de Dios*. I could only look up at the smiling Queen of Heaven at that moment and think that if anyone belonged in Her embrace, it was Glenda Morgan.

I can never hold her again. I will never kiss her lips...but somewhere in this world there is a man who holds Glenda Morgan's light trapped in a tiny bottle. Somewhere there is a man who thinks he can keep her soul as some kind of sick trophy.

My power flows through me now in a steady thrum. Glenda is gone. Jacktown lost a champion that we desperately needed. I have to get in the game. When it comes down to it, all my questions really have been answered. Why was I born a freak? Why was I given these powers?

Simple: because I can help.

I need a license. I have a costume—and thanks to Glenda, I know my name.

You can call me Sacred Heart.

Maybe

Maybe, if someone had been there for him, a few lives could have been saved.

Maybe if someone put her finger to his lips, so that he would know that there was no need to speak...that the time for stumbling words and broken, halting thoughts was over.

Maybe if she touched his mouth like a blind woman, lightly tracing its shape, and smiled. Maybe if her hands spoke a new language, a language of the skin. Maybe if her hands whispered to him:

This mouth of yours is not just a hole. It can do more than let food and pills and whiskey into you, can do more than let pain, and rage, and despair out of you. It can do more than stammer out a memorized banality, more than say the wrong thing, more than grind its teeth with anguish and futility. More.

Maybe if she held his head against her breasts, and wrapped her arms around him, and let him listen to her heart. Maybe if he listened for a long time to the beating of a heart that beat faster for him. Maybe, if she passed soft, soothing fingers over his hard, seething skull...for long enough that his anger could unwind into grief.

Maybe if he was allowed to cry. Maybe if he knew that she would not tell him to stop, or want him to stop, until he was ready to stop. Maybe if he knew that she would never tell anyone, ever, that he was weak.

Maybe if he knew that she would never tell anyone, ever, that he was less than a man.

Maybe if he could touch and squeeze and nuzzle and kiss and suck and bite, and she would not push his hands away or tell him no—even if he hurt her. Maybe if he could feel each rosy point stiffen between his lips and marvel: *this is for me! I am welcome here, I am the one, I have come home at last.* Maybe if he looked up suddenly and saw her solemnly watching, watching him at her breast.

Maybe if she kissed him where it hurt: everywhere.

Maybe if she knelt and took his penis in both her hands and pressed her lips to it reverently, like a Catholic with a holy relic.

Maybe if she opened her arms and took him into her as deep as he would go. Maybe if she didn't care when he was finished, or when she was finished.

Maybe if he knew that she would never tell anyone, ever, that he was less than a man.

Maybe if she stood at the stove and asked: "What's your favorite food?" because she cared what his favorite food was.

Maybe if she tried to make it for him, and it was bad, but he found himself eating it and liking it anyway, because she made it for him.

Maybe if she was there when he got home from the store, and had not run away! Maybe if she had put all his towels in the washing machine instead.

Maybe if she told him all about her small and foolish dreams. Maybe if she trembled when he told her, at last, how they had hurt him. Maybe if she reached out and touched him, and took his hand, smiling bravely and blinking back her tears, when he told her about his ordeal: how he always had to sit alone, eat alone, walk alone. Maybe if he could look into her face and think: *Now I never have to be alone again.*

Maybe if he could face the world and think: *I have someone who loves me and most of you don't.*

Maybe if he gave her some clumsy, awkward gift. Maybe if he realized just as she opened it that it was ugly and shabby and unworthy of her, just like him. Maybe if she put it on right away and would not take it off even when it was dirty, because she was afraid the washing machine would ruin it. Maybe if he realized, slowly, that he had been granted the power to make her happy.

Maybe if he could imagine someone cared, one way or the other, whether he was alive tomorrow. Maybe if she told him how sad it made her to think of people, even bad people, dying before their time.

Maybe if she told him that she was afraid of guns more than anything in the world.

Maybe if he realized how people would point at her and talk, once they shot him down or put him in prison. Maybe if he knew how many times she would sit alone, eat alone, walk alone, because she had been his woman.

Maybe if he knew that once he had done his Great Deed and come to his Great End, the police would come and lock her in a tiny room, and accuse her, hurt her, terrify her. Maybe if he knew that she would be made to cry, for hours, in front of strangers… because she had once opened her arms to him and taken him into her, as deep as he would go.

Maybe if he knew that she would never tell anyone, ever, that he was less than a man.

Maybe then he wouldn't have done it.

Maybe

On the other hand, the little Vietnamese children once looked up to Mark David Chapman with worshipful eyes. And they say that Charlie Starkweather made his girlfriend sit in the car, cold and shivering alone in the dark, while he killed all those people.

Maybe the greatest horror of all is how love really doesn't change anything, when a man is lost.

When Push Comes to Shove

She took him through the alley and up the back stairs to her room, because the man was in rough shape, and the desk clerk was bound to ask questions. It was hard work to get him up to the second floor, but she slung one of his arms around her neck and half dragged him to the top. Even on stiletto heels, she was stronger and steadier than most men.

When the two of them reached the last step, he tried to shake her off. "'M'all right," he mumbled, still holding her scarf to his face. He tugged his right arm free—for the sake of his pride, she let him stagger a few steps alone. Then he reeled again, and put out his hand to catch himself, leaving a smeary red handprint on the wallpaper. She hurried forward to catch him before he fell.

At the door of number 27, she opened three locks and led him inside. The room smelled of soap and oranges. When she flipped the light switch, the bulb flickered to life inside the red sphere of a Chinese lantern.

He mumbled something again as she lowered him carefully onto her bed. She squatted down in front of him and took away his hand, and the scarf that muffled his mouth. "What'd you say, baby?"

"Kindness of strangers," he said, speaking clearly through torn lips. He looked down at her, still holding the bloody clot of silk in his hand. Turned up into the full light, her face was made up into a ghastly whore's mask: lashes heavily lacquered and clumping, lids caked with fuchsia eyeshadow, mouth overwritten with a clumsy pink blotter. Underneath the mask, her eyes were worried and beautiful deep violet-blue.

"That's right," she said, distracted as she took inventory of the damage. "You're a kind stranger, honey." Her voice was soft and husky, but her fingers were firm and professional as she touched the purple mess of his right eye. "Don't worry. Simone is going to fix you up." She stood, tugging her miniskirt back down over her flat rump.

He slumped, holding his side, and closed his eyes against a wave of nausea. Her heels tapped way over a wooden floor and then onto bathroom tile. She turned on the tap, but the water wasn't loud enough to drown out the roar of piss into the bowl.

He nodded off a little; she woke him with the sting of hydrogen peroxide. "Ow," he said mildly. He looked up at her and tried to smile; his teeth were caked with blood and grit.

She shook her head, tossing the brittle curls of a blonde wig. "They sure made a mess of you, honey." She hesitated, holding a pad of gauze in one hand and a bottle of peroxide in the other. "You sure made a mess of them too."

"They had it coming."

Her painted lips trembled. "You mind if I ask why?"

"Why what?"

"Why did you do that? Get into it with those guys?" She soaked the pad again and dabbed at the wound on his forehead; he hissed, cringing away from the sizzle and pain. "I'm a big girl. You didn't have to stand up for me." One of his sad brown eyes rolled toward her, and she read the bemused skepticism there. "There was five of them. They could've killed you."

"They could've killed you too." He gave her his painful smile again. "I had to do it, darlin'. Today was my brother Jimmy's birthday. I was celebrating."

ଔ ଔ ଔ

"Jimmy and I grew up in the mountains," he said. "A shit-kicking little town called Parrot City. It's the asshole of the world. You've never heard of it, unless you're interested in uranium mining or narrow-gauge trains.

"Jimmy was four years younger than me. I loved him. God knows I did. But there was something different about him from the start, and a small town is no place that you wanna be different. By the time he was in the third grade, the bullies were already starting in. He never had an easy time. No matter how many years went by, there was always someone giving him grief.

"Things didn't get bad until high school. I was a senior the same year that Jimmy was a freshman. We were in the same school for the first time since we were little. The same creeps had been after him for years, mind you—but I hadn't actually *seen* them do it since he was eight years old. He was never one to talk about his troubles at the dinner table.

"There was this one asshole in particular that wouldn't let him be. Guy's name was Kirk Royce. Jeezus, what a gorilla. You know the type, I'm sure. The kind of guy who can't just talk shit—he's got to lay his *paws* on you. The guy that gives you his shoulder in the boy's shower, and slams you up against the tiles. The guy who wallops your books out of your arms when you're walking to class. The guy that hip-checks you into a garbage can.

"The day it all came to a head, I was looking for Jimmy in the cafeteria. I don't even remember why. But I saw him coming out of the lunch line with his tray, and I was about to walk up to him, and here comes Royce. He just walks by, reaches out, and gives Jimmy's lunch tray one hard, sudden slap from underneath. Flipped it like a tiddly-wink. My brother is left standing there covered with creamed corn.

"All the goons are laughing, but that's not enough. Royce puts his hand in the middle of Jimmy's chest and just *shoves* him, pushes him so hard that Jim stumbles back and nearly knocks over two other kids with trays.

"'*Watch where you're going, fag,*' he says.

"And Jimmy doesn't say a word. He picks up his empty tray and walks away, while the whole pack of 'em start making noises like a coop full of chickens.

"I shadowed Jimmy to the boy's room. Stood there watching him grind his teeth, trying to get that crap off his shirt and jeans with a wad of wet paper towels.

"'Why do you let him get away with that?' I ask.

"Jimmy rounds on me—and he's as mad as I've ever seen him. 'Get away with what?' he says. 'Pushing me around? The guy is the size of a Buick, Ben. What am I supposed to do about it?'

"'Push him back,' I said. 'He may kick your ass, but at least he won't call you a fag.'

"Jimmy just looked at me. 'Maybe I don't care if he calls me a fag,' he sayd. 'Maybe I am a fag. You ever think of that?'

"That rocked my head back for a second, I must admit. It hit me the way a thing does when you've always known it, but never really thought about it before.

"Half of me just flat denied it. 'He can't be a fag. He's my baby brother, and no brother of mine could possibly be a fag.'

"But the other half of me knew it was true. Jimmy had been queer for as long as I could remember. I just never had a word for the thing that made him different, before.

"'Royce doesn't care,' is what I finally told him. 'It doesn't matter what you really are. He wants a fight, and until he gets one, he's going to get worse.' I handed him my lunch card and looked him in the eye. 'It's another four years 'til you graduate, Jimmy. That's a long time to run.'

"He turned and walked away. I wasn't too surprised; Jimmy never had much use for my advice, when we were growing up. I decided to hang around in the john and have a smoke—the boy's bathroom was one of the few places you could light up without getting caught.

"Soon as I flushed the butt, though, someone came running up to me out in the hall. 'Your brother jus punched Kirk Royce right in the face!'

"So I go to the principal's office and peek in through the glass—sure enough, there's Jimmy, sitting in a chair while they have one of those conversations about whose fist ended up in whose face first. They didn't let him out until just a few minutes before the bell, but when he came out he found me standing there.

"We just looked at each other for a second, and then we both busted out laughing.

"'Since when do you listen to me?'

"'I knocked the sumbitch flat,' he says. 'Put his canine tooth right through his lip—he had to go to the nurse's office.'

"'Serves him right. Now let's hope that this is the end of it.'

"It wasn't, though. Jimmy had detention after school, but so did Royce. I waited around for the extra hour after the final bell rang, because I had a car and I couldn't make Jimmy ride the Activity Bus home. The Activity Bus was the one that ran late, specifically to take the kids who had sports or detention, and it was always full of letterman jackets and juvenile delinquents. The day you finally haul off and punch one of those jock apes in the mouth? You don't ride home in the rolling monkey house. You might just as well paint yourself with barbecue sauce and dive naked into a pit of hogs.

"I met him outside the school and we started walking toward the back lot; that's where I always parked the old station wagon. I could see the jocks out on the football field, twenty or thirty of 'em waiting around in their soccer uniforms, and there was something about the sight that nagged at me. I couldn't quite put my finger on it.

"Jimmy and I had both forgotten that Royce was on the team. Today's detention had made him miss half his practice, and he was plenty pissed. While Jim and I were chit-chatting by his locker, Royce was down in the dressing room suiting up.

"All we heard was a few skipping footsteps across the lot behind us. My reflexes were good, but not good enough; I wheeled just in time to see Royce, running full tilt since he got out the front doors of the school, plant both hands between the shoulder blades of my 135-pound brother and give him a full, football-style block.

"Jimmy didn't just fall, after being pushed that hard. He flew. His feet left the ground and he sailed through the air.

"Royce was two inches taller and at least eighty pounds heavier; delivering the push didn't even slow him down. He kept right on running out to the field, like it was nothing, while Jimmy landed face-down on the asphalt.

"I just stood there as Royce ran away. Looking down at my brother, trying to pick himself up off the asphalt, I felt as if I was seeing him for the first time. It stabbed me in the chest how frail and delicate he was. Just a bony kid with a girl's face, and a soft way about him—a way that would always make some men want to hurt him. The same way some guys want to hurt a pretty girl, when they see her walking by.

"I looked at him, and I realized that he would never be able to push as hard as the world could shove him back.

"I didn't say a word as we walked the rest of the way to the car. I just kept glancing to the side. Every time I looked, I was seeing more. I saw the torn holes in his jeans—thinking my mother would have to patch them. Thinking suddenly of the thousand times she had complained about the way Jimmy tore up his clothes at school. Something in my gut squeezed tight; in those two ragged holes over his knees, I could see a whole echoing history of beatings and bullying that had ripped and torn just about every pair of pants and every jacket he had worn since the seventh grade.

"There were bleeding scratches on his hands. And I couldn't help but think of that painstakingly perfect picture of the P-51 Mustang he drew me for my thirteenth birthday, still hanging above my desk in my room. And how much it would hurt him for the next few days to hold a pencil, even to sign his name.

"Every time I looked at him, I was getting madder.

"'Fasten your seatbelt, Jimmy.'

"As soon as I turned the key in the ignition, it all came clear. The roar of the engine and the roar in my head just seemed to merge. I slowly pulled out and circled the lot, rolling to the farthest corner to give myself a good running start at that field.

"When I floored the accelerator, Jimmy looked over at me suddenly. 'Ben?'

"I didn't answer. I was listening to the crescendo of the engine as we flew across the parking lot. The front tires of the station wagon hit the curb at fifty miles per hour. Two solid tons of Detroit steel, and by God we landed on that field with a crash like thunder.

"When Royce heard the sound, he didn't hesitate—he just ran." The old man gave her a ghastly, bleeding grin. "And that is why he is still alive today, my dear: because he ran, ran like he'd never run before, not in the best game of his best season of his best goddamn year, every time I stomped that gas pedal. I rushed for him again and again, like a mechanical bull. *Toro, toro!*" The old man wheezed laughter.

"The rest of the football team scattered like pigeons in the wind. I could hear a sound like screaming: when I turned I saw my brother James laughing, high and wild, just like a beautiful, evil-hearted woman. Every time Royce spun to the side and dashed out from under the oncoming grille, I took a sod-ripping 180 and went for him again. By the time I was finished, I had torn that field up so bad that they couldn't use it for the rest of the season—and Royce was so played out that he dropped to his knees and covered his face with his hands, waiting for me to end it."

ೞ ೞ ೞ

The man paused, wiping blood from his mouth with the back of his hand. For the first time she felt the need to interrupt him. "Did you kill him?" she said softly. "Did you run him down?"

He gave her a broken smile. "Didn't have to, darlin'. Royce was never going to mess with Jimmy again. Hell, no one did. It was a small town. When you got a crazy brother, the word gets around. I served thirty days in the county jail, but no one in Parrot City ever laid a hand on Jimmy again—he couldn't find a fight with both hands and a flashlight."

He laughed. "Jimmy had to drive thirty miles to get into trouble. When he was eighteen, he took his boyfriend to the senior prom down in Wallisburg; they dressed up in matching cowboy suits, and the farm boys didn't like it I guess. Hell of a fight. He needed thirteen stitches. Who knew that a pair of rawhide chaps could lead to so much carnage?"

He stood, regaining his feet with some effort.

"You don't have to leave," she said.

He shook his head, wincing at the pain in his neck. "No Ma'am. I appreciate the hospitality, but I think you'd best call me a cab. I'll have enough explaining to do when I get home."

She stood silhouetted in the bathroom door, the harsh light spilling over her strong shoulders. "He died, didn't he." It wasn't a question. "That's why you helped me tonight. Because he died."

He sighed. "He would've been thirty-eight years old today. I guess you reminded me of him, when he was younger. Jimmy probably wasn't quite as pretty as you, in a dress, but he did have blonde hair."

"What was it? Fag-bashers?"

"AIDS." He swallowed, turning his face away. "Went down swinging, though. Put up a hell of a fight."

"I'm sorry."

"Don't be sorry, hon." The old man winked his good eye. "Just do me a favor—don't ever let them push you around."

The Passenger

She played it faultlessly, from beginning to end. Meeting at 7:00, just late enough to let him arrive first and pick a spot at the bar. Turning to shrug out of her winter coat, his fingertips brushing her bare neck. Smiles, low-pitched laughter, eye contact. Dinner at 8:30, table manners, questions about his life, his interests, his ideas. A bottle of wine, a sensual dessert, two forks. Another drink, a late-night club with red light and sultry jazz seeping out into the frosty night.

The long warm line of his body pressed to hers, as they danced. The earnest eyes, the firm hand at the small of her back, the playful, lingering kiss.

And then the end. His place, lying on her back at 2 a.m., sweat still drying under the curve of each breast. One arm flung across her forehead. The hammer falling: his return from the bathroom, wearing a pair of pajama bottoms and a sheepish look.

"Look…it's late…"

Closing her eyes, waiting for the rest.

"…and I have to get up early for work."

Quietly she pulled up the sheet. The moment had passed. Now it was necessary to cover herself. She rolled away, avoiding his eyes, and for just an instant there was a stab of longing so powerful that her eyes burned.

I had to leave in a few hours anyway, she thought. *I had to get home and change for work. You could have let me lie beside you, for a few hours.*

"Can I…call you a cab—?"

"No," she said simply. Sitting up, showing him her back. "That won't be necessary."

Swinging her legs over the edge of the bed.

"Are you sure?"

"Yes." Scooping up the crumpled lump of her tights and underwear, still balled into one. Slipping her arms back into her bra.

He turned away to brush his teeth, and she dressed alone. By the time he came out of the bathroom she was already at the door, wearing her coat and gloves, purse slung over one shoulder.

"Good night." He spoke from a distance, still standing on the far side of the room.

She turned back toward him, hand on the doorknob, and forced a smile. "Good night, Paul. And thank you. I had a nice time."

He smiled back. Pure relief: she was going, she was smiling, she wouldn't make a scene.

"Me too." And then, clumsily, "I'll call you."

"That would be nice." Nodding yes. Would be nice. But it wouldn't happen. Holding tight to her thin smile—like the sheet drawn up over her breasts, something necessary to cover herself. She slipped out into the hall, shutting the door softly, letting the pretense drop away instantly. As she pushed the button for his elevator, the rasp of three bolts sounded in the silent hall behind her. His apartment, locked for the night.

She clipped up the empty street, skirting around pools of ice in her low-heeled pumps. The January chill numbed her toes, and crept up her legs like a cold caress. Descending into the stinking cold maw of the subway, she thumbed a token into the turnstile, stepped out onto the platform alone—feeling like the last woman left alive at the end of the world.

She sat in the subway car, roaring through the tunnels beneath the city. She had entered this compartment as the train rolled to a halt, assuming it would be empty—the same reason that she had decided not to take a cab home. If she had to be so incredibly alone, on a night when she had hoped for something more… well, let it be perfect solitude. Unbroken by the nattering of a radio, or a cabby's well-meaning small talk.

Now that she was sitting down, however, it was obvious that she was not alone. There was a second rider at the far end of the subway car, hunched low in the seat.

Homeless, her brain whispered.

It was a muffled mound of gray decay, faceless in the flickering blue light. Brim of a greasy cap pulled down over the eyes. Lank, filthy hair spilling out over the shoulders. Chin vanishing into the coils of a scarf. She had seem them like this before, shuffling slowly around the city—men and women buried in layers of mismatched, cast-off clothing, so far gone that they had degenerated into a walking heap.

Sometimes it was impossible to tell if the person underneath the layers of mildewing cloth was male or female. Equally impossible to tell what they had suffered, what they were still thinking—they had ceased talking, even to themselves. They wouldn't even beg for change anymore. How could you help someone like that?

The Passenger

It must be warmer aboard the train, she thought, and turned away. Warmer than the street. Her own bleak face stared back at her from the window's black glass, her eyes hidden in shadow, two pits in a hollow mask.

The subway squealed, moving slower and slower along the track, and then suddenly halted with a lurch. It was far from any station. A red beacon pulsed somewhere up ahead, bleeding back along the tunnel wall. The overhead lights in the car sputtered and dimmed as the train lost power.

She wrapped her arms around herself, miserable. The moan and growl of other trains echoed all around them in the dark, reverberating in the sudden stillness of the stalled car. A shiver raced across her shoulders, and suddenly, urgently, she wished she had taken that cab—chatty driver and all. Just to be home, at this moment, in her own tiny apartment uptown.

A kettle murmuring on the burner. A bath running in the next room.

Something stirred at the far end of the car, and she stiffened, stealing a sidewise glance at her fellow passenger. The gray mound had risen to its feet. In the dim red glow it seemed bigger somehow. Ominous. Slick soles rasped on the linoleum floor; it was beginning to lurch in her direction.

A sudden, mad urge to run lunged up into her chest. *Don't be ridiculous!* she thought. *It's just a homeless person, for god's sake. Pitiful. Certainly in no shape to HURT anybody.*

And then, more darkly: *run to where?*

Another slow, dragging scrape in the dark. The mound was coming closer, its shabby silhouette filling the aisle. She hugged herself tighter and shrank against the wall.

Maybe...maybe some spare change after all.

Still, she didn't reach for her coat pocket. Because she could smell it now—rotting clothes and rotting flesh and human filth, fouling the air and growing stronger and stronger as the mound continued its slow, painful shuffle.

She was staring at it openly now, frozen in horror and disgust. The light was bad, but there were so many layers...at least two hats, half a dozen coats. The hems of three skirts hanging around the knees. The cuffs of two different pairs of pants, riding one after another, above at least three shades of socks, and—God, even two pairs of shoes, the toes of the smaller pair bursting through the larger, like fresh skin showing through a peeling layer of dead sunburn.

It was standing beside her now, turning toward her slowly. She looked up, to where its face should be, but she could see nothing between the hat and the bile-encrusted scarf—nothing at all.

Her hand shot into her pocket. She pulled out a handful of coins and held them up toward the homeless thing, shaking, quarters and tokens dribbling out between her gloved fingers and rattling away on the floor all around them.

"H-here." Her own voice sounded high and tinny in her ears. "Take it!"

The shuffling mound seemed to stop and dip its head to look down at her outstretched hand. The last two bright coins still winked bright in the palm of her glove. She had risen to her feet now, no longer able to control the instinct that shrieked that she had to get away, as far away from this shambling heap as she possibly could. But she was trapped, her exit from the molded plastic seat blocked by the human haystack. And still she held out that shaking hand... as if she could buy deliverance.

The homeless thing tilted its head back behind the cloaking swathe of scarf. She could see a throat now, a withered mouth hanging open, a single broken tooth. The rotten, ragged arms began to rise from the creature's sides; it was not reaching for her hand, but lifting its sleeves like wings. As the arms opened wide and lifted, the thing's silhouette spread and blocked more of the light. The front of its multiple coats fell open.

She looked down, and for a moment half-expected to see a pitifully shriveled and filthy penis beneath the bizarre layers of clothing. She had lived in the city all her life. Men in overcoats had been exposing themselves to her since she was a child. But what she saw instead was more clothing: shirts beneath sweaters beneath coats.

Despite the low light, she could see a huge black stain had soaked through many layers of fabric. Thick dark spreading blooms over the bulging belly had run down to the knees over a torn polyester skirt.

The smell was thick and overpowering. Her gorge rose and she found herself literally holding her breath, trying not to inhale any more of the corruption. She could feel the cold of the glass and steel behind her seeping through the back of her wool coat. She was pressed tight against the wall of the car, hemmed in by the molded plastic of two seats.

Somewhere in the distant dark, another train was approaching. She looked up suddenly, searching wildly for some salvation in the passing cars on the neighboring track. The other train roared past, its windows still brightly lit florescent blue, and she saw another passenger, a weary face looking out into the dark.

"Help!" she shrieked suddenly, desperately hoping that the person in the passing train would somehow hear. "Help, please!"

On and on she screamed, but the expression on the man's face, the weariness and post-midnight ennui did not flicker with even a spark of doubt or concern.

The subway passed like a rocket, car after blazing car shooting past, and with every cry she seemed to grow weaker. No one heard. By the time the final car vanished around the bend she was openly sobbing.

"Please." Her eyes went back to the silent, motionless creature. She practically moaned the word to the black, bat-winged silhouette standing before her. "Please let me go."

The rumble and groan of the receding train's passage, the reactive creak of the subway car as it rocked and vibrated in sympathy, was almost enough to cover the sound—a bright, crisp rasp of ripping cotton. She looked down at the thing's stomach, following the sound, and saw something black and shining appear. A polished ebony blade, slicing through the layers of cloth from the inside out.

"No." She watched in horror as a second and a third black blade appeared, emerging from the swollen midsection at the center point and slashing outward. The homeless thing tottered forward a step, pushing its way further into her seat as the stained belly and its swaddling of clothes heaved open.

She heard rather than saw the shower of black liquid that rained down onto the linoleum floor. The shredded layers of clothing peeled back in stiffened, brittle curls like the petals of an obscene flower. Inside, a glistening darkness paused, then thrashed wildly as it shook itself free.

The breath had gathered in her throat for a scream, but the sound never came. Instead she heard the crack of a whip. There was a brief stab of pain as the shining stinger unfurled and struck, injecting its poison into the deep well of her bowels. The venom paralyzed her instantly; warm urine splashed down her legs as her bladder went slack. Her legs sagged into wet, useless meat. Her body began to slide slowly down the wall.

As she looked up, she saw the glossy black creature wrench free of its former hiding place. A dozen razor-edged legs, the tips as sharp as needles, slowly unfolded. Protective layers of cloth and flesh, once held tightly shut by those legs as if by surgical staples, gaped open. An oily, segmented body slid out of the gaping cavity of belly and chest, unfurling itself from the empty cavern which should have been packed with human organs.

The thing hooked several of its legs over the rail of her seat and began to kick itself free, ripping and tearing away its rotten prison. Clothing and flesh rained down around her, shaken loose as if the whole heap were crumbling into dust.

The black creature paused, perched on the top of the seat above her. The pulsing red emergency light slid over its gleaming body, the slick needle legs and curving, venomous tail. It shivered in the cold. Unsheathed from its victim it seemed small, delicate.

Vulnerable.

The horror and fear began to leak out of her mind, as if the poisoned numbness of her body were spreading to her brain. With a new and different sense of unease, a more familiar set of feelings and sensations began to seep back into her awareness.

Sad.

A powerful wave of emotion swept through her, and she heard the click of her lover locking the doors against her, at the end of the night. Banished from warmth, from home, from companionship... from simple animal comfort.

Alone.

Pain and longing flared in her chest. Pulling the sheet up over her breasts. Putting on clothes. Clothes. More clothes.

Cover. Protect.

Enveloped in darkness, thin and miserable and pinched by the cold—clutching her coat tightly against the night. Tears slid down her cheeks as she looked up at her fellow passenger, now picking its slow and trembling way down toward her on slim black legs. She felt the warm, slow trail of salt water flowing over her lip and shook with dread. Without warmth, the Passenger would die very quickly. And there was only one place that was

Warm.

Its weight settled on her body. It was heavier than it looked. But no, not as heavy as his body had been, for the brief moment that he had rested, spent and damp with sweat, in her arms....

She heard the tearing sound. Steam rose in a cloud. She sensed the powerful tugging, felt her head lolling this way and that, heard the noisy wet business of its burrowing renovation below the field of her vision. When the fog cleared at last, she found herself on her hands and knees, looking down at her own clumsy hands as they sifted through a scattered pile of cast-off tatters on the floor of the subway car.

The wayward hands found an empty glove, its once-bright colors crusted with filth. She pulled the glove onto her left hand, over the fingers of the black leather kid glove that had been her own. Then her hands went back to their aimless sifting, obedient to the command of the black puppeteer.

A vague sense of curiosity: how many of her inner parts had been removed to make room for the Passenger? How much meat lay abandoned in glistening heaps under the seat? She could feel the flesh drawn tight around her back, the Passenger's needle-like legs threaded through the skin and muscle in front to hold her together, like a coat two sizes too small.

The Passenger

She wondered whether she was still alive, in any real sense of the word. How long would she last? When would the Passenger move on? How long would she remain aware, awake... sharing its thoughts, its feelings?

Somehow, she sensed it would not—could not—be very long.

Never long enough.

Already she could see it coming, the endlessly repeated conclusion to its fruitless search. When at last her body began to collapse into rotten rags, the Passenger would be alone. Once again it would seek out familiar territory. Desolation. Abandonment. Longing.

Homeless and lost, endlessly yearning for something it could never find, it would cast about for someone in the freezing darkness of this barren, horribly alien world that it could recognize as kin—if not in body, then in spirit.

It needed someone to keep it warm, to keep it company. If only for a short while.

But at least, she thought dimly, *it doesn't have to pretend.*

When it's over, no one will make it smile and say thank you, I had a nice time.

The Zombie's Prayer

i still feel it—i do
a little

but nothing hurts
like it should
anymore

the bullets
the blades
they just go
through
and through

a little twitch
like a snagged sleeve
quick movement, deep inside
like a needle sliding out
in the dentist's chair

i stagger
i know
i hurt
but i can only
stumble on…

put a shotgun to my belly
pull the trigger:
tell me that he loves
someone else

and i will fall
to my knees
and weep
or at least
howl...

cold black trickles
running down
my face

i can feel the rage
i can feel the shame
i can see
a gaping tunnel
blasted straight through
me
over which
i grieve

but still i rise
still i move
still i hunger,
helpless
mindless
on and on
and on

the flame-cold power
of seeds in winter
will not let me die

and so
silent
my eyes plead

and my heart whispers
the zombie's prayer:

The Zombie's Prayer

O Great Power
Whose Name i Do Not Know

please, Lord
please…

just let me fall.

About the Author

Arinn Dembo has been a professional writer since 1991. Her articles, criticism and reviews of all popular media have appeared in a variety of print and web publications, and her short fiction and poetry have appeared in *The Magazine of Fantasy and Science Fiction*, *H.P. Lovecraft's Magazine of Horror*, and several anthologies. Since 1996 she has worked as a developer in the computer gaming industry, and her background fiction has enriched a number of popular games for the PC, including *Homeworld*, *Homeworld: Cataclysm*, *Ground Control*, and *Arcanum: of Steamworks and Magick Obscura*. Since 2005 she has been the Lead Writer of Kerberos Productions, an independent game development studio in Vancouver, British Columbia. In that capacity she has continued to write fiction and create new worlds for games, including the apocalyptic milieu of the horror role-playing game *Fort Zombie* and the science fiction backdrop of the *Sword of the Stars* franchise.

She holds degrees in both Anthropology and Classical Archaeology, and lives in Vancouver with her family and a menagerie of pets.

ALSO FROM KTHONIA PRESS

ARINN DEMBO

THE DEACON'S TALE
a Sword of the Stars novel

MILITARY SF FROM THE CELEBRATED LEAD WRITER OF HOMEWORLD, HOMEWORLD: CATACLYSM, GROUND CONTROL, AND SWORD OF THE STARS.

www.ingramcontent.com/pod-product-compliance
Ingram Content Group UK Ltd.
Pitfield, Milton Keynes, MK11 3LW, UK
UKHW041428180426
11947UKWH00007B/341